Smoked Secrets:
Burnt Ends Mysteries

Book 1

Erica J Whelton

Publisher: Sunseri Design Publishing
ISBN: 978-1-956069-38-9

Printed in the United States of America

To my three grandsons who inspired the character Melody.
Keep inspiring me, boys. Gigi loves you.

Chapter One

The fluorescent lights in the law office made everything look sickly green, including Jackie Prescott's complexion as she stared at the papers spread across the mahogany table. She'd read the will three times now, but the words hadn't changed.

"This has to be a mistake," she said, her voice carrying the crisp authority that had served her well in Austin courtrooms for the past fifteen years. "Uncle Charlie Joe barely spoke to our family. Why would he leave us his restaurant?"

Across the table, her sister Lauren shifted uncomfortably in her chair, one hand resting protectively on her daughter's arm. "Maybe because he knew we needed it," she said quietly, then immediately looked like she regretted speaking.

Jackie's eyebrows shot up. "We? I'm doing just fine, thank you."

"Are you?" Lauren's voice carried an edge Jackie hadn't heard in years. "Because from what I hear, your perfect life isn't looking so perfect anymore."

Jackie felt heat rising in her cheeks. Small towns and their gossip networks. "My personal affairs are *none* of your business."

"They are if you're planning to drag us all down with you."

Between them, Melody sat perfectly still, her dark eyes fixed on the ceiling fan's rhythmic rotation. At twenty-two, she had her mother's delicate features and her father's dark hair, but her expression held a focus that most people found unsettling. Jackie had never quite known how to talk to her.

"Ladies," Harold Westin interrupted, his ancient voice creaking like old leather. "Perhaps we should focus on the terms of the inheritance."

"The terms are quite clear," Jackie said, scanning the document again running her finger across as she read. "Both sisters must operate Charlie Joe's BBQ Shack jointly for one full year. If either of us abandons the business or if we fail to work together, the entire property reverts to the state."

She paused to let the words sink in. The only sounds were the low hum of Harold's ancient computer and the tick of a clock on the wall.

"Work together?" Jackie's laugh held no humor. "Harold, we haven't spoken in years. Ever since Mom started her latest drama, when Lauren made it crystal clear she still blames me for choosing sides."

"I don't blame you for choosing sides," Lauren said quietly, but her voice carried an edge. "I blame you for choosing the wrong one. Dad needed us, and you sided with *her* after all she put him through."

"I didn't walk away. I refused to enable his —"

"Don't." Lauren's teacher voice cut through Jackie's response like a blade. "We're not relitigating the divorce here."

The silence that followed was broken only by the soft tapping of Melody's fingers against her jeans. A pattern Jackie couldn't decipher but it seemed to calm the young woman.

"There's more," Harold continued, seemingly oblivious to the tension crackling between the sisters. "The restaurant comes with a two-bedroom apartment above the restaurant. The entire property sits on 12 acres of prime Hill Country land, currently valued at approximately 1.2 million dollars."

Jackie's irritation sharpened into interest despite herself. "What's the catch?"

"You have to live within thirty miles of the restaurant and work there *at least* forty hours a week. Each. For the entire year."

"Forty hours?" Lauren's voice rose. "I can't leave Melody alone for forty hours a week. She needs routine, consistency."

But even as she spoke the words, she knew this could solve a lot of her financial problems. If the apartment is livable, they could give up their ridiculously expensive apartment. Her only concern was changing Melody's routine and life. She'd never done well with changes.

Though Melody was on the spectrum and needed a set routine, for the most part she could be left alone and be trusted not to burn the house down.

Her biggest problem was becoming too hyper focused on something and forgetting to eat or forgetting to take care of her personal needs. She could also be too trusting.

To help herself not be so naïve, Melody had taken it upon herself to study people to help her. She could often be found researching psychology or behavioral articles.

"The restaurant counts as her workplace too, if she chooses to help," Harold said gently.

Jackie studied her sister's worn clothes, the duct tape holding her purse together, the careful way she calculated every expense. "How bad is it, Lauren? Financially, I mean."

"We're managing," Lauren said stiffly.

"That's not what I asked."

"It's none of your business."

"It is if we're supposed to work together."

"Work together?" Lauren's voice cracked slightly. "Jackie, we can't be in the same room for twenty minutes without fighting. How are we supposed to run a business together?"

"Maybe that's exactly why Uncle Charlie Joe did this," Melody said suddenly, her voice clear and precise. Both sisters turned to stare at her. "Maybe he knew you needed each other, even if you don't want each other."

Jackie felt exposed, like Lauren had stripped away all her carefully constructed defenses. How could her sister tell Melody all of her business?

Jackie's hard exterior crumbled a bit.

"Because my perfect life imploded, okay? Richard cleaned out our accounts, my practice is hemorrhaging clients, and I'm starting over at fifty-two with nothing but debt and a bad reputation. My sons are too busy with their own successful lives to care about their mother's problems."

The admission hung in the air between them. Lauren's expression softened slightly, but her voice remained guarded. "I'm sorry. I didn't know it was that bad. How are Alec and Caden handling the divorce?"

"They're not handling it because they're not involved," Jackie said bitterly, but also surprised her sister even knew her sons' names. "Alec's got his medical residency in Seattle. Caden is building his tech company in San Francisco. They send obligatory check-in texts every few weeks, but that's about it."

"That must be hard." Lauren looked over at Melody. She loved her daughter, but she knew that Melody would always live with her. She had no plan for when she died leaving Melody on her own. It was the one thing that kept her up at night. Tomorrow is not guaranteed.

"It's what I raised them for. Independence. Success. I just didn't realize that success would mean they wouldn't need me anymore." Jackie turned back to Harold. "What exactly does 'fail to work together' mean in legal terms?"

"Physical abandonment of the business, documented refusal to cooperate, or any action that demonstrably undermines the restaurant's operations."

"And if one of us quits?"

"The entire inheritance goes to the state. The other sister gets nothing."

Lauren and Jackie stared at each other, the weight of their mutual dependency settling over them like a heavy blanket.

"So, we're stuck with each other," Jackie said finally.

"Looks like it," Lauren replied.

"This is going to be a disaster."

"Probably."

Melody cleared her throat. "Actually, the mathematical probability of success is quite good, assuming you can both prioritize the business over your personal conflicts."

"That's a big assumption," Jackie muttered.

"I want to see the restaurant," Melody announced. "Before we make any decisions, I want to evaluate the operational systems and assess whether this venture is viable."

"She means she wants to see if Uncle Charlie Joe was as organized as she is," Lauren translated with the first genuine smile Jackie had seen from her all day.

Jackie's attention was suddenly caught by something else entirely.

"Harold," she interrupted, "what exactly did Uncle Charlie Joe die of?"

The old lawyer shifted uncomfortably. "Natural causes. He was seventy-three, had some health issues."

"What kind of health issues?" Jackie's legal instincts were fully engaged again. "And who determined it was natural causes?"

"Well, the local doctor, Dr. Thorne. Said it was his heart."

"Dr. Thorne," Jackie repeated. "Related to the Thorne family that runs the general store?"

"His son, yes. Dr. Michael Thorne. Been the only doctor in Prairie Rose for about fifteen years, took over the practice when old Doc Williams retired." Harold looked increasingly uncomfortable. "But Jackie, I don't see why —"

"When did Uncle Charlie Joe last see a doctor? When was his last physical? What medications was he taking?" Jackie was in full cross-examination mode now.

Harold looked increasingly uncomfortable. "I don't have those details. Dr. Thorne said it was sudden but not unexpected given Charlie Joe's age and his recent complaints about chest pains."

"Recent complaints?" Lauren asked. "When recent?"

"Dr. Thorne mentioned that Charlie Joe had come in a few weeks before his death, worried about heart palpitations and shortness of breath. Said he'd advised him to reduce stress and consider retirement." Harold shuffled through his papers. "The doctor felt Charlie Joe's death was consistent with untreated cardiac stress."

"But there was no autopsy?" Jackie pressed.

"Dr. Thorne felt it was unnecessary given Charlie Joe's recent medical complaints and the clear symptoms of cardiac arrest. Said an autopsy would just be an expensive formality that wouldn't change anything."

Lauren was looking at Jackie with growing concern. "What are you thinking?"

"I'm thinking that people don't usually write wills leaving property to estranged family members when they're planning to live for years," Jackie said slowly.

Melody looked up from her contemplation of the ceiling fan. "Statistical probability of sudden cardiac death in males over seventy is approximately 8.2 percent annually. But the timing, immediately after writing a will that would transfer his property to family, that's statistically unusual."

"Melody's right," Jackie said. "The timing is suspicious."

"Jackie, you're reading too much into this," Harold said firmly. "People get their affairs in order when they feel mortality approaching. It's completely normal."

"Maybe. But I'd like to see the death certificate. And I'd like to know who was the last person to see Uncle Charlie Joe alive."

Harold sighed and reached for a file cabinet. "If it will put your mind at ease." He pulled out a folder and handed Jackie a copy of the death certificate. "As for who saw him last, that would be Jovie Barber, his cook and only steady employee. She found him when she came in to open the restaurant that morning."

Jackie studied the death certificate carefully. It was sparse on details but the cause of death was listed as "acute myocardial infarction," time of death estimated between 11 PM and 1 AM, body discovered at 5:30 AM.

"So, who made the decision not to do an autopsy?"

"The family," Harold said, then paused. "Well, since Charlie Joe had no immediate family, I suppose it was Dr. Thorne's recommendation and the sheriff's decision."

"Sheriff Martinez?"

"No, this was before Ray Martinez was elected. Sheriff Henderson was still in office. He retired just days after Charlie Joe's death."

Jackie felt pieces of a puzzle starting to form, but the picture of what it should be was unclear. "Where is former Sheriff Henderson now?"

"Moved to Florida, I think. Retired and sold his house here."

"That's not unusual," Lauren said, though she sounded less certain. "Lots of people retire to warmer climates."

"Lauren," Jackie said slowly, "what if Uncle Charlie Joe didn't die of natural causes?"

"What do you mean?"

"I mean what if someone killed him? Maybe that's why he suddenly wrote a will leaving everything to us? Because he knew someone was circling his property or his life or something," Jackie said.

The room fell silent.

"That's a very serious accusation," Harold said finally.

"It's a very serious possibility," Jackie replied. "And I think we need to investigate it."

Lauren studied her sister. She could see the determination in her eyes. If she were honest with herself, she was curious to find out why he left this to them as well, and could it be that he was murdered?

"I'm in."

"Me too," Melody added.

"Does that mean you have decided to keep the business?" Harold asked hopefully.

"It's a huge commitment so I would still like to check it out before we make a final decision," Jackie said looking to her sister for confirmation.

Lauren simply nodded.

"Okay, just let me know. I have a lot of interested parties asking about the property, but Charlie Joe wanted it to go to family. His exact words were family first." Harold nodded.

"Who was interested in it?" Jackie asked.

"Investors, development companies, other restaurants looking to expand. I've told them all any bids would have to wait until the family decided on what they would do with it first."

As they gathered their things to leave, Harold cleared his throat one final time. "Ladies, Charlie Joe asked me to give you this advice: the secret to good barbecue isn't in the recipe. It's in the patience."

"Patience," Lauren repeated. "The one thing neither of us has ever been good at."

"Especially with each other," Jackie added.

Outside the law office, they stood awkwardly beside their cars. Jackie's three-year-old SUV next to Lauren's ancient Honda that looked like it was held together by hope and duct tape.

"So," Lauren said finally. "Are we really going to do this?"

"I don't see that we have much choice," Jackie replied. "Unless you want to walk away from 1.2 million dollars."

"I can't walk away from that much money," Lauren admitted. "Melody's future depends on it."

Jackie looked over at her niece who was now seated in the car tapping her fingers. She couldn't hear the sound but knew it must be the same pattern Melody had been doing in the office just minutes before.

"And I can't afford to walk away from any money right now." Jackie admitted.

"So, we're both trapped."

"Completely trapped."

They looked at each other. Thirty-five years of hurt and misunderstanding stretched between them.

"We're going to kill each other," Lauren said quietly.

"Probably," Jackie agreed. "But maybe we should at least look at the restaurant first, so we know what we're fighting over."

"Okay. Meet you there." Lauren turned to her car.

As they drove along the gentle hills covered with live oak, cedar trees with cacti dotted along the road toward Prairie Rose, Jackie couldn't shake the feeling that Uncle Charlie Joe had orchestrated this entire situation. Somehow, he'd known that neither sister could afford to walk away, ensuring they'd be forced to confront not just his legacy, but each other.

The question was whether they'd survive the experience intact or destroy each other in the process. Not to mention what they were walking into.

Chapter Two

The hand-painted sign had seen better days. The wood was weathered gray, and the letters spelling out "Charlie Joe's BBQ Shack" were faded but still legible in cheerful red paint. Below it, a smaller sign declared "Best Brisket This Side of Heaven" in Uncle Charlie Joe's careful script.

Jackie pulled into the gravel parking lot and killed the engine, staring at the building through her windshield. It wasn't as bad as she'd feared, but it wasn't good either.

The structure was basically a large wooden box with a covered porch running along the front. String lights hung between the posts, half of them dark. Mismatched picnic tables sat scattered across the porch and under a massive oak tree that dominated the front yard.

Lauren's Honda crunched to a stop beside her, and Jackie watched in the rearview mirror as her sister and Melody climbed out. Melody immediately walked to the oak tree and stood beneath it, her head tilted back to study the canopy of leaves.

Jackie watched her for a moment, curious about what the girl was looking for. Melody had that same focused stare as she'd had in the lawyer's office.

"Well," Jackie said to herself, "here goes nothing."

She got out of the SUV and was immediately hit by the lingering smell of smoke and meat that seemed to permeate the very air around the building. It wasn't unpleasant but more welcoming and almost comforting. The rich and complex smell with hints of oak and hickory made her stomach growl despite her anxiety.

"The smell is consistent," Melody announced from under the tree. "Smoke particles have settled into the wood grain of the building. That means years of regular use with proper temperature control."

Lauren smiled at her daughter. "That's a good sign, right?"

"It means Uncle Charlie Joe knew what he was doing," Melody said. "Inconsistent smoking creates uneven odor dispersal. This is very even."

Jackie raised an eyebrow. "How do you know that?"

"I researched barbecue techniques after we got the inheritance notice," Melody said matter-of-factly. "I read seventeen articles and watched forty-three YouTube videos. Knowledge reduces anxiety."

"Of course you did." Jackie found herself almost smiling. Maybe having Melody around wouldn't be as challenging as she'd thought.

Harold had given them three keys on a ring shaped like Texas. The front door was painted bright blue and had a small window covered with gingham curtains. Jackie inserted the first key and turned it.

The door swung open with a soft creak, and they stepped into Charlie Joe's BBQ Shack.

The interior was dark until Lauren found the light switches. Fluorescent fixtures flickered to life, revealing a space that was both larger and smaller than Jackie had expected.

The dining area held maybe a dozen tables; each covered with red-and-white checkered tablecloths that had seen better days. The walls were covered with old photographs, newspaper clippings, and what appeared to be thirty years' worth of customer testimonials written on index cards and tacked to a corkboard.

"Oh my," Lauren breathed, walking toward the far wall. "Look at this."

Jackie followed and found herself staring at dozens of photographs of Uncle Charlie Joe with customers. In every picture, he wore the same outfit: jeans, a white t-shirt, and a sauce-stained apron that read "Pit Boss." His hair had gone from dark brown to silver over the years, but his smile remained constant. It seemed genuine and a little shy.

"He looks happy," Lauren said softly.

"He looks tired," Jackie countered, but even she could see the contentment in their great-uncle's eyes.

Melody had wandered toward the kitchen area, which was separated from the dining room by a long counter with a pass-through window. "The organization system is logical," she called out. "Consistent spacing between tables. Clear sight lines from the kitchen to all seating areas. Efficient traffic flow patterns."

Jackie joined her at the counter and looked into the kitchen. It was small but immaculate, with everything in its place. Stainless steel prep tables, a large refrigerator, and a gas stove that had probably been installed in the 1990s. On the wall, a laminated chart showed cooking times and temperatures for different cuts of meat, all written in Uncle Charlie Joe's neat handwriting.

"Where's the actual barbecue pit?" Lauren asked.

"Out back," Jackie said, remembering Harold's brief description. "The real cooking happens outside."

They found the back door and stepped onto a covered porch that ran the length of the building. And there it was, Uncle Charlie Joe's pride and joy. The smoker was enormous, a black steel barrel the size of a small car with a firebox attached to one side. The metal was seasoned to a deep black patina that spoke of years of careful use.

"It's beautiful," Melody said, and Jackie was surprised to hear genuine awe in her voice. It was the first sign of an emotion she'd seen from the girl all day.

"It's a machine," Jackie said.

"It's both," Lauren corrected, running her hand along the smoker's surface, surprised to find it still warm. "Look how well-maintained it is. Not a spot of rust anywhere."

Lauren turned with a smile. Her enthusiasm was so contagious that even Jackie had a giddy flutter in her stomach.

This could work, she thought.

Besides the main smoker, there was a smaller upright unit, a large propane grill, and storage areas for wood and supplies. Everything was organized with the same attention to detail she'd noticed in the kitchen.

"The wood supply is precisely stacked," Melody observed, pointing to neat rows of split logs. "Oak and hickory separated by type and size. Each stack contains approximately the same amount of wood. Uncle Charlie Joe was very systematic."

"How can you tell the difference between the woods?" Jackie asked.

"Bark patterns, grain structure, color variations," Melody said, as if it were obvious. "I researched that too."

They spent a few minutes exploring every corner of the restaurant and immediate area. The walk-in cooler was spotless and well-organized. The dry storage area contained industrial-sized containers of rubs and sauces, all labeled with expiration dates in Uncle Charlie Joe's handwriting. Even the bathrooms were clean, with fresh soap and paper towels.

"I hate to admit it," Jackie said finally, "but this place is in better shape than I expected."

"It's more than that," Lauren said. "It's loved. Look." She pointed to a small herb garden beside the back porch, where rosemary, basil, thyme, and a few other herbs grew in neat rows. "He was still taking care of this place right up until the end."

Jackie felt an unexpected pang of sadness. She'd barely known Uncle Charlie Joe, but walking through his restaurant felt like getting to know him. Every detail spoke of a man who took pride in his work and cared about his customers.

He'd sent cards at Christmas and birthdays, and there were some memories of him when they were very young girls, but outside of that, they didn't know him.

Jackie looked over at her younger sister. Life is short. Would she regret the past thirty-five or so years if something happened to her?

"There's something else," Melody said. She was standing by a small office door they hadn't noticed before. "This door doesn't match the others."

Jackie looked where Melody was pointing. She was right. The office door was newer, with a different lock and a small security camera mounted above it.

"Why would he need a security camera just for his office?" Lauren wondered.

"Because there's something in there he wanted to protect," Jackie said, trying the second key from the ring. It fit perfectly.

But their exploration of Uncle Charlie Joe's mysteries was interrupted by the sound of hoofbeats. A man on horseback approached from the neighboring pasture, riding along the fence line that separated the restaurant property from rolling hills dotted with cattle.

He was weathered and lean, probably in his fifties, wearing a sweat-stained hat and boots that had seen decades of honest work. His horse was a sturdy quarter horse with intelligent eyes, but there was something in the rider's posture that suggested barely controlled anger rather than casual neighborliness.

Jackie quickly relocked the office, shoving the key into her pocket as the trio went outside to meet the cowboy. They crossed to the far side of the property just as he reached the fence line.

"Y'all must be Charlie Joe's family," he called out, dismounting with practiced ease, but his tone carried an edge that immediately put Jackie on alert. "Tom Whitfield. My family owns the land that borders yours. It has four generations."

Jackie approached the fence cautiously, noting how the man's eyes moved systematically over their property with the calculating gaze of someone who knew every acre intimately. "Nice to meet you, Mr. Whitfield. I'm Jackie, this is my sister Lauren and her daughter Melody."

"Nice to meet ya. You can call me Tom," Tom said, his handshake firm and slightly too long, as if he were marking territory. "My great-grandfather settled this area back in 1892. Built the first ranch house, dug the first wells, ran the first cattle. Course, that was before certain... complications arose."

"Complications?" Lauren asked.

Tom's jaw tightened. "Your great-uncle bought land that should have stayed in our family. My granddaddy had a handshake agreement with old Thorne to sell that land to us when he was ready. Been negotiating for months, had the financing arranged, even had the survey done."

"But Uncle Charlie Joe made a higher offer?" Jackie asked.

"Charlie Joe came in with cash and bought it out from under us in a single day," Tom said, his voice carrying decades of resentment. "Never gave us a chance to match the offer, never even acknowledged our family's history with this land."

He gestured toward the creek that wound through Uncle Charlie Joe's acreage. "That water source has been keeping our cattle alive during drought years since my great-grandfather's time. Charlie Joe never understood what it meant to ranching families who've been working this land for over a century."

"I'm sorry that happened," Lauren said diplomatically. "That must have been frustrating for your family."

"Frustrating doesn't begin to cover it," Tom replied, his hand resting on his belt in a way that made Jackie notice the knife sheathed there. "Cost us half our herd during the drought of 2011. Had to sell prime breeding stock, take out loans we're still paying on. All because a stranger with suspicious money bought land that belonged with our ranch."

"Suspicious money?" Melody asked, looking up from her systematic examination of the fence line.

"Cash deals that size don't happen in legitimate business," Tom said. "Always wondered where Charlie Joe got that kind of money so quick-like. Man shows up out of nowhere, pays cash for prime Hill Country land, never talks about his past. Makes a person curious about what he might be running from."

"Did you ever ask him about it directly?" Jackie asked.

Tom's smile was cold. "Asked him plenty of things over the years. About his water usage, about his business practices, about whether he'd consider selling back what rightfully belonged to our family. Charlie Joe was always polite but never accommodating. Said the land was his legal property and that was the end of it."

"Legal property," Melody repeated thoughtfully. "But you believe it should have been your family's property."

"I know it should have been," Tom said firmly. "My daddy spent twenty years trying to buy that land fair and square. When he died five years ago, one of his last requests was that I keep trying to reunify our family's original ranch holdings."

The way he said "keep trying" made Jackie's skin crawl.

"Well, we appreciate you introducing yourself," she said, trying to end the conversation. "We're still getting acquainted with the property and the business."

"Of course, of course. Y'all take your time figuring things out." Tom remounted his horse, but his expression remained calculating. "Just know that if you ever decide this restaurant business isn't working out, my family would be very interested in discussing a sale. We'd pay fair market value, cash deal, and we'd be grateful to finally restore our ranch to what it was meant to be."

"We're not looking to sell," Jackie said firmly.

"Things change," Tom said with a shrug that didn't reach his eyes. "Business can be unpredictable. Equipment breaks down, customers disappear, sometimes folks realize they're in over their heads. When that happens, it's good to have neighbors who understand the value of the land."

The threat was subtle but unmistakable. Jackie felt Lauren step closer to her, creating a united front.

"We appreciate the... neighborly concern," Jackie said coolly. "But we're committed to continuing Uncle Charlie Joe's legacy."

Tom's expression hardened. "Charlie Joe's legacy is complicated. Man kept to himself, didn't participate in community affairs, never supported local ranching interests. Some folks might say his legacy isn't worth preserving."

This was in stark contradiction to all the pictures displayed within the restaurant, but Jackie believed he was trying to intimidate them. She'd seen it plenty in courtrooms.

"What folks?" Melody asked with her characteristic directness.

"Folks who remember what this land was like before Charlie Joe isolated it from productive agricultural use," Tom replied. "Folks who understand that twelve acres of prime ranch land shouldn't be wasted on a small-time restaurant when it could be supporting sustainable cattle operations that benefit the entire community."

"The restaurant benefits the community too," Lauren said. "People come here, spend money, gather with friends and family."

"City people," Tom said dismissively. "Tourists looking for authentic Texas experiences they can Instagram. They don't understand what real ranching communities need to survive."

As Tom prepared to leave, he paused and looked directly at Jackie. "Y'all seem like nice ladies, but this is hard country. Sometimes it's not safe for people who don't understand local customs and relationships. Charlie Joe learned that lesson eventually."

"What do you mean?" Jackie asked.

"I mean Prairie Rose takes care of its own, but it doesn't always take kindly to outsiders who don't respect established ways of doing things." Tom touched his hat brim in a gesture that somehow managed to seem threatening rather than polite. "Hope y'all figure out how to fit in better than Charlie Joe did."

As he rode away, Jackie felt a chill that had nothing to do with the afternoon breeze.

"That felt like a threat," Lauren said quietly.

"It was definitely a threat," Melody confirmed, making notes in her journal. "His body language shifted significantly when I challenged his economic assumptions. Increased tension in facial muscles, altered vocal patterns, defensive posturing."

"You think he's dangerous?" Jackie asked.

"I think he wants this land very badly," Melody replied. "And I think he's not used to people who can match his arguments with actual data."

Lauren was staring after Tom's retreating figure. "Did you notice how he knew exactly which areas had the best grass, where the water sources were, how the drainage worked? He's been studying this property for a long time."

"More than studying it," Jackie added grimly. "Planning for it."

"Since we were interrupted, should we explore the outside, maybe check out this water that Tom was so interested in?" Lauren asked.

"Absolutely," Jackie said.

They continued their exploration of the property, but the encounter with Tom Whitfield had changed the atmosphere. What had felt like inheriting a charming family business, even though they still hadn't decided on it, now felt more complicated, more contested.

The twelve acres were beautiful with its rolling hills covered with native grass and wildflowers, the ancient oak trees providing shade and character, the creek meandering through it all like a ribbon of life. Limestone and granite rocks jutted from the ground and in the creek causing swirls and ripples as the water rushed over them.

But Jackie now saw it through different eyes. This wasn't just land; it was valuable land that other people wanted. Harold had already mentioned it, and someone had potentially killed to try to get it.

"Look at this," Melody called from near the creek bank. She was examining the ground with her usual methodical attention. "There are tire tracks here. Recent ones. And footprints."

Jackie and Lauren joined her. Sure enough, someone had driven back here recently, probably within the last few days. The grass was flattened where a vehicle had parked, and several sets of footprints were visible in the soft earth near the creek.

"Could this have been Mr. Whitfield?" Melody asked.

"No. He was on horseback," Jackie said.

"Maybe it was Harold, checking on the property?" Lauren suggested.

"Maybe," Jackie said, but something about the scene bothered her. The tire tracks were wide, suggesting a large truck or SUV. The footprints showed at least two different people, and they'd spent considerable time here. The prints were numerous and overlapping.

"Or maybe someone else has been poking around," Lauren said. "Didn't Harold mention something about a lot of interest in the property?"

"Yes, he did," Jackie said, looking around. "Let's head back."

As they walked back toward the restaurant, Jackie found herself looking at the property with new awareness. The peaceful Hill Country setting suddenly felt less isolated and more vulnerable. The restaurant sat far enough from the main road to provide privacy, but that same privacy could be a liability if someone with bad intentions came calling.

But as they approached the restaurant's back door, Jackie couldn't shake the feeling that they were being watched. She glanced toward the fence line where Tom Whitfield had disappeared but saw only empty pasture and grazing cattle.

Still, the feeling persisted. Someone was interested in this property, interested enough to drive back here and look around, interested enough to make veiled threats about land use and tradition.

Uncle Charlie Joe had installed security cameras for a reason. And Jackie was beginning to suspect that the reason might still be relevant.

"Come on," she said to Lauren and Melody. "Let's see what other secrets Uncle Charlie Joe left for us to find."

As they unlocked the back door, Jackie's phone buzzed with a text message. Unknown number.

Nice place you've inherited. Be a shame if something happened to it.

She stared at the screen, her blood running cold.

"What is it?" Lauren asked, noticing her expression.

Jackie showed her the phone.

Lauren read the message and paled. "Is this some kind of joke?"

"I don't think so." Jackie looked around the peaceful property with new eyes. "I think we're not the only ones interested in Charlie Joe's BBQ Shack."

"We knew that," Lauren said. "Do you think this is Tom Whitfield?"

"Maybe," Jackie said, looking towards the property line again.

"What do we do?" Lauren asked.

"We go in here and see what's in that office," Jackie said, opening the back door.

As they stepped into the restaurant's kitchen, Jackie realized that inheriting Charlie Joe's BBQ Shack was going to be more complicated than any of them had imagined.

The question was whether they were strong enough to handle whatever complications lay ahead, and whether they could work together.

Looking at her sister and niece, seeing the determination in Lauren's eyes and the analytical curiosity in Melody's expression, Jackie felt a surge of something she hadn't experienced in years.

Not just confidence, but family solidarity. Whatever Uncle Charlie Joe had gotten them into, they'd face it together.

Even if it meant standing up to neighbors who thought they knew what was best for the land, investigators who asked too many questions, and secrets that had been buried for thirty years.

Chapter Three

They were halfway across the dining room when the front door burst open with a bang that made all three women jump. A thin, willowy woman in her sixties strode in like she owned the place, her gray hair pulled back in a practical ponytail. She looked like a strong wind could blow her over but moved with the confidence of someone who'd never backed down from a fight.

She was loaded down with grocery bags and immediately headed to the counter area where the cash register sat.

"Well, I'll be damned," she said, setting the grocery bags down and quickly moving behind the counter to the cash register.

Her hands moved swiftly over the machine. Jackie couldn't tell if she was opening it, closing it, or checking something, but there was a practiced familiarity that seemed almost secretive.

Jackie instinctively stepped in front of Lauren and Melody, her lawyer instincts kicking in. "I'm sorry, but we're closed. The restaurant isn't —"

"Closed?" The woman let out a bark of laughter, stepping back around to the front of the counter, but not before Jackie noticed her slip something small into her apron pocket. "Honey, Charlie Joe's never been closed a day in thirty years, and I'm not about to let it start now." She extended one hand toward Jackie. "Jovie Barber. I'm the cook, bookkeeper, and whatever else needs doin' around here. Been running the place alone for the last two months since Charlie Joe... well, since his passing."

Jackie hesitantly shook the offered hand, which despite belonging to such a slight woman, was surprisingly strong and calloused. But she couldn't shake the feeling that Jovie's behavior around the cash register had been deliberately evasive.

Harold had mentioned her, but he left out the part that Jovie was still running Charlie Joe's BBQ Shack. That would have been good information to know before they arrived.

"I'm Jackie Prescott, and this is my sister Lauren Beniot and her daughter Melody."

"I know who you are," Jovie said, but there was something calculating in her tone. "Charlie Joe talked about you girls. Worried about you too, especially after he heard about Lauren's situation." She nodded toward Melody. "Single mom, special needs daughter, no steady income. Charlie Joe understood what that was like to have a family member who needed expensive care."

"What do you mean?" Jackie asked, her attorney instincts now fully alert.

"Oh, my daughter Emma. She's been fighting cancer for the past three years." Jovie's voice grew tight. "Good insurance, but you know how it is. Experimental treatments insurance won't cover, copays that add up to more than most people make in a year."

"That must be incredibly difficult," Lauren said sympathetically.

"Charlie Joe helped when he could," Jovie said, glancing back toward the cash register. "He gave me advances on my salary, let me work extra hours for extra pay. Of course, running this place alone the last two months, I've had to... make some adjustments to keep things afloat."

"What kind of adjustments?" Jackie asked.

"Just creative bookkeeping," Jovie said quickly. "Nothing dishonest, mind you. Just... prioritizing which bills get paid when. You understand. A business can't run itself, and medical bills don't pay themselves either."

Jackie filed away this information about Jovie's financial pressures and her convenient access to the restaurant's finances for the past two months.

She walked across the room and pointed at a small picture. They followed her to look at it closer. There was a faded picture of two little girls. One with pigtails and the other with a huge toothy grin. It was a picture they'd missed while assessing things earlier.

"Here look at this. Charlie Joe kept tabs on family, even if he didn't visit."

"That's us," Lauren said, then looked at another. "This one is Melody. Oh, gosh, I'd forgotten I'd sent him this one."

"He worried about how the family split affected you girls, especially when he heard Lauren was struggling and Jackie was too proud to help."

Jackie's jaw tightened. "That's not... it's more complicated than that."

"Is it?" Jovie asked mildly. "Or are you both still fighting the same fight you started more than thirty-five years ago?"

Lauren flushed. This woman sure knew a lot about them for being a stranger to them.

"Uncle Charlie Joe knew about all that?"

"Honey, Charlie Joe knew about everything. Your parents' divorce, Steve's getting remarried, how Dawn's still bitter about it all, the sides you picked, how it tore you apart." Jovie's voice softened slightly. "He also knew you were both too stubborn to fix it on your own."

Her knowledge of them was startling, but Jackie had other things on her mind.

"Jovie, how long have you been managing the restaurant's finances?" Jackie asked, recalling how quickly the older woman had moved to close or adjust the cash register when they'd first entered.

"Oh, for years. Charlie Joe hated that part of the business, so someone had to keep track of the money." Jovie's voice was casual, but she didn't meet Jackie's eyes.

"Must have been a lot of responsibility, especially running this place the last few months alone," Lauren said sympathetically.

"A blessing, really. He would want the business to go on and I knew you girls would show up soon. Plus, I needed the extra work, and Charlie Joe paid me well for the extra tasks I took on." Jovie paused, then added quietly, "Medical bills don't pay themselves."

Something in her tone made Jackie's attention sharpen, and she also noted how Jovie kept glancing back toward the cash register area, as if making sure everything was secure. The behavior struck her as more than just protective. It seemed almost guilty.

"We're just looking around," Jackie said, filing away this information about Jovie's financial pressures. "We haven't decided whether to accept the inheritance yet."

Jovie stopped and turned around, fixing Jackie with a look that could have melted steel. "Haven't decided? Do you have any idea what this place meant to your uncle? What it means to this community?"

"It's a restaurant," Jackie said defensively.

"It's a lifeline," Jovie corrected. "You know how many people Charlie Joe fed for free when they couldn't pay? How many kids got after-school jobs here when nobody else would hire them? How many folks came here just to have somebody to talk to?"

"That's very noble," Jackie said, "but it's not a sustainable business model."

Jovie pointed to a photo showing Uncle Charlie Joe serving a plate of food to an elderly man. "See this? That's Frank Kowalski. He comes in every Tuesday and Friday for lunch. He's been a widower for five years, and those are the only hot meals he gets all week. Charlie Joe never charged him full price."

She moved to another photo. "This is Maria Santos and her three kids. She works two jobs, and sometimes Charlie Joe would 'accidentally' make extra food that needed to be taken home before it spoiled. Her kids are mostly grown now, but he was still helping her out."

Jackie felt something uncomfortable twisting in her stomach. "That's not how you run a profitable business."

"There she goes," Lauren muttered. "Everything's about profit margins with you, isn't it?"

"Someone has to think about reality," Jackie shot back. "You can't run a business on good intentions."

"And you can't build a community by treating people like balance sheet entries," Lauren replied.

"Ladies," Jovie interrupted, but both sisters were warming up to their argument.

"This is exactly why this won't work," Jackie said to Lauren. "You think with your heart instead of your head."

"And you think with a calculator instead of considering actual human beings," Lauren replied, her voice rising.

"At least I think! You just react emotionally to everything."

"Better than being a cold, calculating —"

"Stop." Melody's voice cut through their argument like a blade. Both sisters turned to stare at her. "You're fighting about management philosophy when you don't even know what you're managing yet."

Jovie was watching this exchange with interest rather than alarm. "Smart girl," she said approvingly. "Your uncle would have liked that attitude."

Melody blinked. "Are you here every day?"

"Yep, seven days a week," Jovie said, turning to face Melody directly. "Tuesday through Sunday the restaurant's open. Mondays I do the shopping." She gestured to the pile of groceries still on the table. "It's the only day of the week we aren't open, but we smoke each and every day."

"That's a good schedule," Melody said approvingly. "Consistent. Do you follow the same routine each day?"

"Pretty much. Arrive by five, start the fires, prep the vegetables, check the meat, begin the smoking process." Jovie studied Melody with growing interest. "You like routines?"

"Routines are efficient. They minimize variables and reduce the possibility of errors."

"What do you mean you start the fires?" Jackie asked to get them back on topic. "Don't you just turn on the smoker?"

Jovie stared at her like she'd suggested they microwave the brisket. "Turn on the smoker? This is real barbecue. Wood fire, careful temperature control, hours of attention. You don't just flip a switch. Real Texans will know the difference between that fake smoke and the real deal."

"Speaking of neighbors," Jackie said, trying to sound casual, especially since nobody had actually said anything about neighbors, but the mention of 'Real Texans' had her remembering the one on horseback. "We met Tom Whitfield earlier. He seemed very interested in our property."

Jovie's expression immediately grew guarded. "Tom Whitfield's been sniffing around this place for twenty years. Always making offers, always suggesting Charlie Joe was getting too old to run a restaurant, claiming his family had first dibs on buying this property, which if you ask me is a bunch of bull hockey."

"What kind of offers?" Lauren asked.

"Low-ball offers. Way below market value. Tom's been in financial trouble for years what with the drought killing most of his herd a year ago. He hasn't recovered yet and the bank's been pressuring him." Jovie walked to the window and peered out toward the fence line. "Charlie Joe always said Tom would try to get this land one way or another."

"Did Uncle Charlie Joe ever feel threatened by him?" Jackie asked, thinking about the text message she'd received only minutes ago.

"Not threatened exactly, but... annoyed. Tom could be persistent. Sometimes he'd show up unannounced, wanting to 'discuss options' for the property." Jovie's voice carried a note of disapproval. "Charlie Joe was polite about it, but he told me once that Tom seemed to know an awful lot about the restaurant's business for someone who was supposedly just a neighbor."

"What do you mean?" Melody asked, looking up from her notes.

"Tom always seemed to know when we had a slow week, when equipment needed repairs, when Charlie Joe was feeling poorly. Like he was keeping track of our weak spots." Jovie turned back to face them. "It made Charlie Joe uncomfortable, having someone watching that closely."

Jackie filed this information away. Between Tom Whitfield's land grab ambitions and Jovie's financial desperation, there were already multiple people with potential motives if something had happened to Uncle Charlie Joe.

"Do you think it was just about the land and water? Or do you think it was about something else?" Lauren asked.

"What do you mean?"

"Did he seem interested in the business perhaps?"

"Now there's something I didn't think of. Maybe that's it," Jovie said.

Jackie had to admit her sister was quite intuitive. It was an angle that she hadn't seen herself. If he was in debt, maybe he was eyeing the restaurant as a quick money maker to help him pay back the bank.

"How many hours?" Melody asked Jovie, interrupting Jackie's thoughts.

"How many hours for what? Smoking?" Jovie asked.

"Yes," Melody said.

"Brisket takes twelve to fourteen hours, depending on the size. Ribs take six. Pulled pork anywhere from eight to twelve." Jovie walked to the pass-through window and pointed to the chart on the kitchen wall. "Charlie Joe's timing chart. Every cut of meat, every cooking temperature, every variable you need to know."

Jackie felt overwhelmed just looking at the complexity. "And you do all this by yourself?"

"Charlie Joe and I worked great as a team. This last year, he mostly handled the customers while I did the cooking." Jovie's voice grew softer. "He was proud of this place. Proud of the food, proud of the people who came here. He'd be heartbroken to see it sitting empty."

But even as Jovie spoke about Uncle Charlie Joe's pride, Jackie noticed how the older woman had positioned herself near the cash register again, and how her eyes kept darting toward the office door. There was something about Jovie's body language that suggested she was more nervous than she was letting on.

"It won't be sitting empty if we sell it," Jackie said practically.

"To be torn down for condos," Lauren said bitterly. "That's your solution to everything. Sell it and walk away."

"That's not fair."

"Isn't it? When things get difficult, you bail. Just like you did with Dad, just like you did with our family."

"I didn't bail on anything. I made practical decisions based on realistic assessments." Jackie's nose flared.

"You abandoned us," Lauren said quietly, but her words carried the weight of thirty-five years of pain.

"I didn't abandon anyone. I just didn't want to enable —"

"There you go again with that word. 'Enable.' Like caring about people is some kind of weakness."

Jovie cleared her throat loudly. "Ladies, much as I'm enjoying this family therapy session, you need to make a decision."

Lauren and Jackie looked at each other for a second. The years of not speaking. The years of pain. It all came down to this decision, but before they could discuss it further, there was a loud bang from somewhere outside.

"Someone's at the smoker," Jovie said, her voice tight with anger. "Nobody touches Charlie Joe's smoker without permission."

But as she moved toward the back door, Jackie noticed that Jovie didn't seem surprised by the interruption. In fact, she moved with the purposeful stride of someone who had been expecting this.

They followed her to the back door. Through the window, they could see a figure in dark clothes doing something to the main smoker unit.

"Hey!" Jovie shouted, throwing open the door. "Get away from there!"

A man in a baseball cap pulled low over his face looked up. For a moment, he stood frozen. Then he dropped whatever he was holding and ran toward the tree line.

"Stop!" Jackie called, but the man disappeared into the woods.

Jovie was already examining the smoker, her face growing darker by the second. "That bastard put sugar in the firebox and partially dismantled some of the grates," she said. "Sugar burns too hot and too fast which could start a fire and ruin the unit."

"Sabotage," Lauren said quietly.

"More than that," Jovie said grimly. "This is a warning. Someone really doesn't want you girls to keep this place running."

"Did you recognize him?" Lauren asked.

"No, not a bit."

But Jackie was watching Jovie carefully now, noting how quickly she'd assessed the damage, how she seemed to know exactly what to look for. "Jovie, how do you know so much about what was done to the smoker? You examined it for maybe thirty seconds."

"I... I've been working with this equipment for twenty years. I know when something's wrong."

The sabotage temporarily united the sisters in alarm, but Jackie's suspicions about Jovie were growing stronger.

"The threatening text," Lauren said looking at her sister, unaware of Jackie's growing distrust of Jovie.

Jovie's expression hardened. "What threatening text?"

Jackie hesitated a moment before showing her the message. Jovie read it twice, her frown deepening.

"Son of a biscuit," she muttered. "I knew this would happen."

"You knew?" Jackie asked sharply.

"Charlie Joe was worried about it. Last few months, he had people sniffing around. Not just one greedy neighbor, but developers, real estate agents, folks asking about his plans for the property."

"What did he tell them?"

"Same thing he told everybody. The restaurant would stay in the family." Jovie looked at the three women, but Jackie noticed she was studying their faces more than seemed necessary. "Question is, are you family enough to keep it?"

"I think we are," Jackie said. She didn't like the idea of being threatened. Not by Jovie, not by some neighbor and not by whoever had sent the text. It made her blood boil and the urge to fight rose within her. She examined the damage. "But this is serious."

"Should we call the police?" Lauren asked.

"And tell them what? That someone put sugar in our smoker?" Jackie shook her head. "We need more evidence before —"

"We need to get out of here," Lauren interrupted. "This is too dangerous, especially with Melody."

"So, you want to run away," Jackie said. "Just like Dad, just like always."

"I want to protect my daughter, and Dad didn't run away. Mom kicked him out."

Jackie ignored the part about their parents. "By teaching her that the solution to every problem is to give up and run?"

"By teaching her that some risks aren't worth taking."

"And by teaching her that when things get tough, family abandons each other?" Jackie crossed her arms.

They stared at each other across the damaged smoker, years of resentment and misunderstanding crystallizing in this moment.

"I never abandoned you," Lauren said quietly.

"You chose Dad's side knowing it would hurt me."

"You chose Mom's side knowing it would hurt me."

"And here we are," Jackie said bitterly. "Still hurting each other."

Melody, who had been quietly examining the sabotage, suddenly looked up. "Uncle Charlie Joe knew this would happen."

"What?" Both sisters asked.

"Not the sabotage specifically. But the fighting. The inability to work together." Melody studied them both with her analytical gaze. "That's why he structured the inheritance the way he did. He knew you'd both be forced to stay and work it out instead of walking away from each other again."

"Work what out?" Jackie asked.

"Whether you love each other more than you hate each other," Melody said simply.

The words hung in the air between them like a challenge.

"We don't hate each other," Lauren said finally.

"Don't we?" Jackie asked. "Because it feels like hate sometimes."

"It feels like hurt," Lauren corrected. "It feels like thirty-five plus years of hurt that we've never dealt with."

Jackie stared at Lauren. She couldn't argue with Lauren's assessment. It was hurt, not hate. She swallowed hard, then turned to look at the damaged smoker.

Jovie, who had been watching this exchange with what seemed like more than casual interest, finally spoke up. "Well, you can hash out your feelings later. Right now, you've got a decision to make. Are you going to let whoever did this scare you off, or are you going to fight?"

"I vote fight," Melody said unexpectedly. "This place is worth fighting for. And so is family."

Jackie looked at her sister, at her niece, at the restaurant that Uncle Charlie Joe had loved enough to leave them despite knowing they'd probably kill each other trying to run it. She also looked at Jovie, who claimed to care about Uncle Charlie Joe's legacy but who had financial pressures, access to everything, and knowledge that seemed to go beyond what an employee should have.

"I guess the question is," Jackie said slowly, "are we brave enough to find out if Uncle Charlie Joe was right about us?"

"Right about what?" Lauren asked.

"That we're stronger together than apart. Even if we can barely stand each other most of the time."

Lauren stared off into the distance then finally she nodded toward the damaged smoker. "Someone really doesn't want us here."

"All the more reason to stay," Jackie said, surprising herself.

"Are you sure? Because I can't do this alone, and I won't watch you bail out the first time things get really difficult."

"I won't bail," Jackie said. "But I also won't pretend this is going to be easy."

"It's going to be hell," Lauren agreed.

"Probably."

"We might actually kill each other."

"It's possible."

They looked at each other for a long moment, both acknowledging the enormity of what they were committing to.

"Well," Jovie said with a grin that didn't quite reach her eyes, "Charlie Joe always did like a good challenge. Let's get to work."

As they began assessing the damage to the smoker, Jackie realized that Uncle Charlie Joe's real gift wasn't the restaurant or the land. It was the opportunity to either fix their broken relationship or destroy it completely.

The question was which one they'd choose.

But she also realized they'd need to be very careful about who they trusted. Between Tom Whitfield's land grab ambitions and Jovie's suspicious behavior, they were surrounded by people who had their own agendas.

And one of those people might be willing to kill to get what they wanted.

Chapter Four

It took them three hours to clean the sugar out of the smoker, and by the time they finished, Jackie's manicured nails were ruined and her back ached from hunching over the firebox. But the satisfaction of seeing the unit restored to working order surprised her.

"Not bad for a beginner," Jovie said, examining Jackie's work on the grates. "You might actually have a knack for this."

"Don't sound so shocked," Jackie muttered, wiping sweat from her forehead with the back of her hand. "I'm not scared of a little hard work."

Melody had taken charge of getting the groceries put away and then organizing the wood supply, arranging the logs by type and size with military precision.

"The previous system was adequate," she announced, "but inconsistent spacing created inefficient airflow patterns. This arrangement will optimize combustion."

"She's been reading about barbecue physics," Lauren explained, watching her daughter with pride and amusement. "I found her watching YouTube videos about heat transfer at two in the morning."

"Smart girl," Jovie said approvingly. "Charlie Joe would have *really* loved having someone who understood the science behind the art."

Jackie's phone buzzed from a number she recognized as Harold Westin's office.

Another party interested in making you an offer on the property. Cash deal, closing in 30 days. Thought you should know. - HW

She showed the message to Lauren, who paled.

"They're sure persistent. Why?" Lauren asked.

"There's a lot of money involved, and at a million and a half for the land alone, the sharks are circling. It could be worth more if they want the water rights too, like Tom does," Jovie said grimly.

Hearing it again, Jackie felt dizzy. That much money would solve all her problems and set Lauren and Melody up for life. But looking around the restaurant, seeing the photos of Uncle Charlie Joe with his customers, she felt that uncomfortable twisting in her stomach again.

She knew that they couldn't sell, even though every instinct in her said to cut her losses and get back to her normal life, or what was left of it.

"There's something else you need to know, likely related to the threatening text and the sabotage," Jovie said quietly. "Charlie Joe wasn't just worried about developers. He was scared."

"Scared of what?" Lauren asked.

"He didn't really say much but it started about six months before his death. Phone calls, unexpected visits, people following him home. I found him more than once whispering on the phone." Jovie's voice dropped to almost a whisper. "Day before he died, he told me he was thinking about closing the restaurant and disappearing again."

"Again?" Jackie caught the word immediately.

Jovie looked like she'd said too much. "Charlie Joe had a complicated past. Let's leave it at that."

"No," Jackie said firmly, her lawyer instincts fully engaged. "If we're going to make a decision about this place, we need to know what we're getting into. What did Uncle Charlie Joe mean by disappearing again?"

"I honestly don't know all the details, but what I do know is he left his old life, spent a year traveling around before settling here."

"Okay, so he was hiding from something is what you are saying?" Jackie asked.

"Yep. Seemed like it, and I wouldn't be surprised if he wasn't … murdered."

Both sisters gasped. Lauren looked to see where Melody had wandered off to and had she heard. It was always hard to tell what her daughter heard and understood because she never gave a clue until she would blurt out her thoughts on the conversation.

"I thought he died of natural causes. A heart attack." Jackie said half question and half statement. She'd already had doubts about how he died and voiced those concerns in Harold's office, but hearing Jovie say this was almost validating.

"That's what they want to think. People in town that is. And, yes, he had been aging, slowing down a bit, and had a few health issues, but nothing that should have killed him so quickly. But nobody wants to investigate it as murder. Not in Prairie Rose. Tourists are our lifeline, so we can't have word of a potential murderer on the loose," Jovie said.

Lauren's face paled. She couldn't put Melody in danger. Her daughter was naïve and couldn't distinguish between a friend or foe.

"I was ready to sign on for this, but Melody …"

"I'm fine, Mom. I want to do this," Melody appeared behind her.

"But … " Lauren wanted to argue but knew she wanted to do this more. No. It was more like she needed to do this. She had no choice. Money was getting tighter by the day. This at least had earning potential, even if it was small. "Fine. What time do we all meet tomorrow?"

"Five AM," Jovie said.

Jackie hesitated. She'd been planning to drive home, sleep in her own bed, and maybe reconsider this whole crazy venture in the morning. With an hour and a half drive each way, she would have a short night.

But looking at the restaurant they'd just committed to saving, she felt an unexpected reluctance to leave. She also had the sudden protective urge over her sister and niece. It was an unfamiliar feeling after all the lost years.

"I should probably stay," she said slowly. "In case whoever sabotaged the smoker comes back."

Jovie raised an eyebrow. "I figured Miss Lawyer would be heading back to Austin."

"The drive is long, and I have a feeling I'll be too exhausted to do it twice a day."

"Well okay. You can use the apartment above the restaurant," Jovie offered. "It's not fancy, but it's clean."

"What about you?" Jackie asked Lauren. "Where are you staying?"

"We have a motel room in town," Lauren said, though she really wanted to save the money. She just didn't want to admit that to Jackie. She'd made the reservation before she knew about the apartment and the drive home was more than two hours north. "It's fine for a few nights while we figure things out."

"A motel?" Jackie looked at her sister's worn clothes, her duct-taped purse, the careful way she'd been calculating every expense. "How much is this costing you?"

"It's fine," Lauren said quickly, the same defensive tone she'd used since they were kids whenever money came up.

"Lauren —"

"I said it's fine." But Lauren's voice cracked slightly on the last word.

Melody spoke up. "The two bedrooms are nice sized. I checked them out earlier. Plenty of space to live temporarily to reduce costs and improve security."

Both sisters stared at her.

"That's actually not a bad idea," Jovie said. "Safety in numbers, and you'd both be here early for the morning prep."

Jackie felt panic rising in her chest. Share living space with Lauren? They could barely manage to be in the same room for a few hours without snapping at each other, but she knew her sister needed to save money.

"I don't think ..."

"It makes financial sense," Melody continued with her usual logic. "Mom's budget is stretched, and Aunt Jackie's going through a divorce. Shared expenses would benefit both parties."

"Since when do you know about my divorce budget?" Jackie asked.

"Since you mentioned how your life imploded, legal bills and starting over," Melody said matter-of-factly. "Also, your car payment is probably more than Mom's monthly rent, but you're driving a four-year-old SUV instead of new, which suggests financial constraints."

Lauren looked at Jackie. She wanted to speak up but didn't know what to say.

"I'm not having money problems," Jackie said defensively. "I'm just... reassessing my priorities."

"Because Richard cleaned you out," Jovie said bluntly.

Jackie whirled around. "How do you ... why would you say that?"

"Small town. Word travels. Plus, Charlie Joe mentioned it last time we talked." Jovie's expression softened. "He was worried about you too, you know. Said you'd been putting on a brave face, but that divorce was eating you alive."

Jackie felt her carefully constructed walls beginning to crumble. She'd already had an outburst and admitted too much in Harold's office but knowing Jovie knew was too much.

Uncle Charlie Joe had known about Richard's affair, about the financial devastation, about the humiliation of having her perfect life exposed as a facade.

He probably even knew about how distant her relationship with her sons had become, how success had taught them they didn't need their mother anymore.

"The apartment has a full-sized bed in one room and two twins in the other," Melody said, apparently oblivious to the emotional undercurrents. "Adequate sleeping arrangements. Mom and I can share the room with the two twin beds."

"Are you comfortable with this change?" Lauren asked.

"Yes, I want to stay," Melody said simply. "The routines here are comforting. And I think Uncle Charlie Joe left us something important to discover."

"What makes you think that?" Jackie asked.

"Someone went to considerable trouble to sabotage the smoker. People don't typically invest that much effort unless the stakes are significant. And if Uncle Charlie Joe was killed to protect this, we owe it to him to find out why and what." Melody's voice grew more animated.

Jackie hadn't seen much emotion from her niece until now. It caused Jackie to get almost excited too.

"She has a point," Jovie said. "Charlie Joe was paranoid about something those last few months. Kept talking about protecting the family secrets."

"What family secrets?" Lauren asked.

"That's what we need to find out," Jovie said. "But not tonight. Tonight, we get some rest, and tomorrow we learn how to smoke brisket."

Jackie looked at the text message again from Harold. "Let's get one day behind us before we make a final decision."

"Maybe two," Lauren said.

As the sun began to set, painting the Hill Country in shades of gold and orange, Jackie found herself standing in Uncle Charlie Joe's apartment, holding a small overnight bag she'd retrieved from her car. She was always one to be prepared, even if her initial plan had been to drive home.

More than once she'd got caught in a courtroom or client meeting away from home and had to stay the night. That's when she started always traveling with a bag.

The space was simple but comfortable with a kitchenette, a living area and two small bedrooms with a bathroom between them. Everything was clean but a thin layer of dust had accumulated since his death.

She watched her sister go into one of the two bedrooms with Melody and her bag, so she went into the other to set her own bag down.

Lauren was unpacking Melody's carefully organized suitcase in one of the bedrooms, while Melody explored every corner of the apartment with her usual systematic attention. This could be perfect for her and Melody, but a bit crowded with Jackie here too.

She could do anything short-term if it meant saving money. It was temporary until they figured out their plan. Then she'd find something more permanent.

"The shower has good water pressure," Melody announced. "And the kitchen is adequately stocked with basic supplies."

"Thank you for the housing report," Jackie said dryly.

"You're welcome," Melody replied, missing the sarcasm entirely.

Lauren emerged from the bedroom and found Jackie staring out the window at the darkened restaurant below. "You don't have to stay if you don't want to," she said quietly.

"I know that." Jackie replied without looking at her.

"So why are you?"

Jackie was quiet for a long moment. "Remember when we were kids, and Dad would take us fishing at the creek behind Grandma's house?"

"Long before the divorce," Lauren said carefully.

"Before everything fell apart," Jackie corrected. "You always wanted to catch the biggest fish, and I always wanted to catch the most fish."

"And we'd end up arguing about who won."

"But we were still fishing together." Jackie turned to face her sister. "I haven't felt like part of a team in a long time. Maybe not since then."

Lauren's expression softened. "Jackie... "

"Look I'm not saying this fixes anything between us," Jackie added quickly. "We still have a lot to work through. But maybe Uncle Charlie Joe was smarter than we gave him credit for."

"Maybe," Lauren agreed. "Though I still think he's crazy for believing we can run a restaurant."

"The mathematical probability of success is actually quite good," Melody said, appearing in the doorway with a notebook. "I've been calculating our assets and liabilities."

"Of course you have," Jackie said, a smile spreading across her face. She was getting used to Melody's quirks. They were endearing.

"Our main advantages are Jovie's expertise, the established customer base, and the prime location. Our main disadvantages are lack of experience and the threat of sabotage." Melody consulted her notes. "However, if we can maintain current revenue levels and minimize additional costs, we should achieve profitability within six weeks."

"That's assuming no one burns the place down," Lauren said.

"The probability of arson is difficult to calculate without more data about our antagonist," Melody said seriously.

Jackie felt a laugh bubbling up in her chest, the first genuine laugh she'd had in months. "Did you just say 'antagonist'?"

"It's the correct term for someone working against the protagonist's goals," Melody said with dignity.

"And we're the protagonists in this scenario?"

"Obviously. We inherited the restaurant, we're trying to save it, and someone is attempting to stop us. Basic narrative structure."

Lauren was smiling too. "She's been reading mystery novels," she explained. "She says they help her understand human motivations."

"And do they?"

"Sometimes," Melody said. "Though people are generally less logical than fictional characters, which makes them harder to predict."

"So, what are we going to do?" Lauren asked.

Jackie looked around the apartment that Uncle Charlie Joe had called home, thought about the customers whose photos lined the restaurant walls, and considered the family secrets they had yet to uncover.

"We get up at four-thirty tomorrow morning," she said. "We learn how to smoke brisket, and we figure out what Uncle Charlie Joe was so afraid of and if it got him killed."

"And if our antagonist escalates their efforts?" Melody asked.

Jackie smiled grimly. "Then they're going to discover that Rodriguez women don't scare easily."

"We aren't Rodriguez," Melody said.

"That was our maiden names, and you are part of me, so that makes you one too." Lauren smiled at her daughter. "Many people still refer to us as Rodriguez."

Melody seemed satisfied with that answer and began tapping as she went back to exploring the house. Jackie focused on the pattern trying to decipher it.

"It is the rhythm or beat of a song I would sing to her as a baby. It's part of her stimming," Lauren explained.

"Ah, I have heard of that."

"Yeah, some kids flap their arms. Some spin. They're all different, that's why they say spectrum. Well one reason."

Jackie watched Melody for a moment longer, before calling it a night.

As she settled into the full bed an hour later, listening to the old building creak and groan around them, Jackie couldn't shake the feeling that they were missing something important. Someone was very determined to get them off this property, and she doubted it was just about real estate development.

Uncle Charlie Joe had been scared enough to consider disappearing again. What had he known that they didn't?

And more importantly, what lengths would someone go to in order to keep it buried along with him?

Tomorrow, she thought. That's when they would start getting answers. One way or another.

Chapter Five

The alarm went off at 4:30 AM, and Jackie seriously questioned every life choice that had led her to this moment. She rolled out of bed with a groan, her back protesting from the unfamiliar mattress and the previous day's physical labor.

"Coffee," she mumbled, stumbling toward the kitchenette.

"Already brewing," Melody said cheerfully from the tiny dining table, where she sat with a notebook and what appeared to be a half-dozen hand-drawn flowcharts. "I've been awake since three, reviewing Jovie's instructions and optimizing our workflow."

Lauren emerged from the bedroom looking only slightly more human than Jackie felt. "Please tell me you found coffee."

"Melody beat us to it," Jackie said, pouring two mugs of the strongest coffee she'd ever smelled.

With the coffee in hand, she walked over to see what Melody had been working on so diligently. She picked up one of the many flowcharts, studying it closely. It appeared to be the schedule for the day.

Jovie had given her the schedule yesterday before she left during Melody's questioning.

"What time do you start the brisket?" Melody had asked, pen in one hand, a notebook in the other.

"Five AM," Jovie replied. "Ideally though it would be best to cook it overnight. That's what Charlie Joe used to do. Now I have to serve today's briskets tomorrow."

"And the ribs?"

"Seven AM."

"Sides?"

"Eight thirty."

Melody nodded, processing the information. "I could learn that schedule. It's logical and predictable, and we can work on figuring out the overnight brisket with time."

She had scribbled it all down, and this morning had turned it into a comprehensive diagram.

Lauren came to stand next to her, looking over her shoulder. "I used to buy dozens of notebooks and reems of drawing paper so that Melody could do this growing up. I have boxes of flowcharts and notes."

Jackie looked at her and then over at the artist. Melody was reading over her notes comparing it to one of the flowcharts. She had a meticulous, logical way of looking at the world.

It was amazing. Why had Jackie always thought this was a disability? This was special.

"This is all so exciting," Melody said.

"Exciting?" Lauren took a sip of coffee. "Honey, you know we have no idea what we're doing, right?"

"That's what makes it interesting," Melody said. "New challenges require new neural pathways. It's stimulating."

Jackie studied her niece. "You're not nervous at all?"

"I'm terrified," Melody said simply. "But terror and excitement create similar physiological responses. I've chosen to interpret the signals as excitement."

"That's actually pretty wise," Jackie said.

"Thank you. I read it in a psychology article about reframing anxiety."

A knock at the door interrupted their conversation. Jovie stood on the landing, looking impossibly alert for someone who'd supposedly been up as early as they had.

"Morning, ladies. Ready to learn how to make magic?"

"Magic?" Jackie asked.

"That's what Charlie Joe called good barbecue. Said the transformation from raw meat to perfect brisket was the closest thing to magic most people would ever witness."

They trooped downstairs to the restaurant, where Jovie had already begun assembling ingredients. The morning air was crisp and cool, perfect for smoking, according to the weather app on Jackie's phone.

"First lesson," Jovie said, leading them to the outdoor kitchen. "Fire is not your friend. Fire is your partner. You respect it, you understand it, but you never trust it completely."

She demonstrated how to build the fire in the smoker's firebox, explaining the difference between seasoned oak for steady heat and hickory for flavor. Melody took notes furiously while Lauren and Jackie watched Jovie's practiced movements.

"Temperature control is everything," Jovie continued, checking the thermometer built into the smoker. "Too hot and you dry out the meat. Too cool and you might as well be cooking pot roast. We want steady heat between 225 and 250 degrees."

"How do you maintain that for twelve hours?" Lauren asked.

"Practice, patience, and good wood," Jovie said. "Plus, checking every hour or so, adjusting as needed."

"Did you learn all of this from Uncle Charlie Joe?" Lauren asked.

"Yes, from him and he learned from Ezra Hutchins."

"Oh, I heard stories about him and there were pictures of them downstairs."

"He had been a mentor and a good friend to Charlie Joe from the minute Charlie Joe arrived in Prairie Rose."

The next two hours passed in a blur of instruction. They learned how to select brisket ("Look for good marbling and consistent thickness"), how to trim fat ("Leave about a quarter inch for flavor and moisture"), and how to apply the dry rub ("Charlie Joe's secret recipe").

By seven AM, they had six briskets, twelve racks of ribs and four pork shoulders in the smoker along with chicken and sausage. Jovie explained that the longer meats would be cooked then stored to be served the next day.

Jackie's hands were coated with spice rub and her hair smelled like smoke, but she felt oddly satisfied. She smiled with contentment at a job well done that she hadn't felt as a lawyer.

"Not bad for beginners," Jovie said, watching Jackie carefully monitor the smoker temperature. "You're getting the hang of it."

"It's like a science experiment," Melody observed, making another note in her book. "Variables must be controlled and monitored for optimal results."

"Exactly right," Jovie said. "Now comes the hard part."

"What's that?" Melody asked with genuine curiosity and pen poised to take notes.

"The waiting. Good barbecue can't be rushed." Jovie chuckled.

Jackie watched in amusement as Melody wrote it down.

They moved inside to prep the sides, and this was where things started to fall apart.

Their first real argument erupted over the coleslaw. Lauren wanted to follow Uncle Charlie Joe's traditional recipe exactly, hand shredding cabbage and measuring ingredients by eye. Jackie demanded precise measurements and wanted to use a food processor.

"We're not changing his recipe," Lauren said firmly, reading from a card in Uncle Charlie Joe's handwriting.

"The recipe calls for hand shredding the cabbage. This is incredibly inefficient," Jackie protested. "We could save twenty minutes with a food processor. There has to be a faster way."

"Speed isn't the point," Lauren said. "The process is the point."

"The process doesn't pay the bills."

"Neither does rushing and ruining the food. Plus, hand-shredded has better texture," Lauren said.

"Hand-shredded is labor-intensive nostalgia that will put us out of business."

"It's what Uncle Charlie Joe wanted."

"Uncle Charlie Joe is dead, Lauren. We're the ones who have to make this work in the real world."

The words hung in the air like a slap. Lauren's face went white, and for a moment, Jackie thought her sister might walk out entirely. If she could take it back, she would but that's not how words worked.

"I know he's dead," Lauren said quietly. "I also know he built something beautiful here, and you want to turn it into another soulless corporate operation."

"I want to turn it into a profitable business that can actually support three people instead of a money-losing tribute to a dead man's nostalgia."

"And I want to honor the man who believed in us enough to leave us his life's work."

"Well, we can't do both," Jackie snapped. "So, which is it going to be, sentiment or survival?"

"Why can't we do both?"

Jackie gritted her teeth. "Fine. We'll try."

She just hoped that Melody could come up with a more efficient way to do things and prove that hand shredding was a waste of time.

When their first customers arrived at 11:00 AM on the dot, the tension between them was so thick it could be cut with a knife.

They watched as the elderly man climbed from his truck, the door squeaking so loudly it could be heard inside. Jackie's nerves were on edge and that sound nearly sent her over it.

"That's Frank Kowalski," Jovie said quietly. "Tuesday regular. He always orders a chop brisket sandwich, extra sauce and pickles with a sweet tea."

"The man from the photo," Lauren remembered. "The one Uncle Charlie Joe never charged full price."

"Yes exactly," Jovie said firmly. "Charlie Joe would haunt this place if we changed that."

Jackie felt her business instincts rebel, but she nodded. "What do I need to know about taking orders?"

"Be friendly, don't hover, and remember that most folks come here as much for the conversation as the food."

Frank Kowalski entered to find both sisters behind the counter, radiating hostility. His warm smile faded to a deep frown.

"Everything all right, ladies?" he asked cautiously.

"Fine," they said simultaneously, then glared at each other.

The lunch service was a disaster from that moment on. Jackie tried to optimize every process while Lauren insisted on personal service for every customer. They stepped on each other, argued over orders, and generally made a mess of what should have been simple operations.

"Order up!" Jovie called, but neither sister was at the pickup window.

"Where's the sweet tea for table three?" Lauren called.

"I thought you were managing drinks," Jackie replied.

"When did we decide that?"

"When you said I was too corporate to understand customer service!"

"Ladies," Frank Kowalski interrupted gently, "maybe I could just grab my own tea?"

Both sisters rushed to help him, colliding in their haste and spilling coleslaw across the floor. Several customers exchanged uncomfortable glances. A few, who hadn't yet ordered, turned and left without a word.

"This isn't working," Jackie said through pursed lips, trying to keep up the facade, but it was fooling no one, as they cleaned up the mess.

"You think?" Lauren replied sarcastically.

Somehow they made it through the lunch service despite themselves.

"We better take advantage of the lack of customers to clean and check on the smoker," Jackie suggested.

They began wiping tables, emptying trash bags, but then Jackie noticed Jovie at the cash register, this time openly counting money and making notes in a small ledger.

"How did we do today?" Lauren asked.

"Better than I expected," Jovie replied, but she closed the ledger quickly when Jackie approached. "Course, there are still expenses from the last few months that need sorting out."

"What kind of expenses?" Jackie asked.

"Oh, you know. Supplier payments, utility bills, payroll." Jovie's hands moved protectively over the ledger. "Charlie Joe wasn't always... systematic about his record-keeping toward the end. I've been trying to piece things together."

"I'd like to review the books," Jackie said. "Get a sense of our financial position."

"Of course, of course. Just give me a few days to organize everything properly. You don't want to see the mess Charlie Joe left behind. It would just confuse things."

"I thought you had been keeping the books the past year or so," Jackie said.

"Oh, yes, I was but Charlie Joe liked to do some too. Just give me a few days, I promise."

Melody, who had been quietly observing this exchange, made a note in her ever-present notebook. Jackie caught her eye and saw the same suspicion reflected there.

By 2 PM, they'd served only eighteen customers instead of their planned thirty, received three complaints about slow service, and were both ready to kill each other.

"We're terrible at this," Lauren said, slumping into a chair.

"We're terrible at this together," Jackie corrected. "I could run this place efficiently if I didn't have to coordinate with someone who thinks feelings matter more than logistics."

"And I could create a welcoming atmosphere if I didn't have to work with someone who treats customers like data points."

"Both of you could succeed if you stopped trying to prove you're right and started trying to make it work," Melody said firmly. "You're so busy competing with each other that you're sabotaging the business."

"We're not competing," Lauren protested.

"You are. You're competing to be right about how to run the restaurant, who Uncle Charlie Joe would have preferred, who understands the community better." Melody consulted her notebook. "You've contradicted each other twenty-three times today, revised each other's decisions fifteen times, and spent more energy arguing than cooking."

They didn't reply to her. Jackie crossed her arms hard over her chest while Lauren stared in the opposite direction.

Melody flipped a page in her notebook. "I've identified several efficiency improvements we could implement."

"Such as?" Lauren asked.

"The ordering process creates bottlenecks. We could streamline by grouping similar items and optimizing the pickup flow. Also, the cash register system is outdated and slows transaction processing."

"You want to redesign our workflow after one morning?" Jackie asked.

"I want to optimize it," Melody corrected. "The current system works but isn't efficient, especially if you two can't work together."

"She's not wrong," Jackie admitted, her shoulders droopy in defeat. They had to do something different.

They put the argument aside as they discussed Melody's suggestions when the front door chimed. A man in an expensive suit walked in, looking completely out of place among the rustic décor.

"Can I help you?" Lauren asked.

"I hope so," the man said with a practiced smile. "I'm Harrison Kale from Kale Development. I believe your lawyer mentioned I might be stopping by."

Jackie felt her hackles rise. This was one of the developers who'd been circling like a vulture, waiting for them to give up.

"We're not interested in selling," she said curtly, even though they had not officially said they were keeping it. She didn't need to tell this stranger.

"I understand completely," Kale said smoothly. "New business, lots of work, probably overwhelming. I'm just here to make sure you know you have options."

"We know our options," Jackie said. "There is only one we are considering, and that's keeping the restaurant."

Kale's smile never wavered, but Jackie caught something cold in his eyes. "Of course. I just wanted to mention that my offer has a time limit. Development permits, you understand. If you change your mind, I'll need to know within the next two weeks."

"We won't change our minds," Lauren said firmly stepping closer to her sister trying to create a united front. Despite their differences, they had the same goal.

"Things happen," Kale said with a shrug. "Equipment breaks down, customers disappear, accidents occur. Sometimes people realize they're in over their heads."

The threat was subtle but unmistakable. Jackie stood up, using her full height and courtroom voice. "Mr. Kale, I think you should leave now."

"Absolutely," he said a smirk spreading across his face. "Just remember, my door's always open. For now."

After he left, the sisters sat in angry silence. Angry from their fight and angry from the visitor.

"Maybe he's right." Jackie exhaled heavily. "Maybe we should just sell and split the money."

"Is that what you want?" Lauren asked.

"I want to be realistic about our limitations."

"Our limitations, or your unwillingness to compromise?"

"My unwillingness to compromise? You're the one who won't modernize anything, who insists on doing everything exactly the way Uncle Charlie Joe did it even when it doesn't work!"

"And you're the one who wants to turn this place into a McDonald's with better meat!"

"At least McDonald's makes money!"

"Money isn't everything, Jackie!"

"It is when you don't have any!"

They were shouting now, thirty-five years of hurt and resentment pouring out in the empty restaurant.

"You know what?" Jackie stood up abruptly. "Maybe we should quit. Maybe Uncle Charlie Joe was wrong about us. Maybe some things are just too broken to fix."

"Fine," Lauren said, standing also. "Sell the place. Take your half of the money and go back to Austin. Run away like you always do when things get difficult."

"I don't run away. That's you."

"Really? What do you call choosing Mom over Dad? What do you call moving to Austin instead of staying close to family? What do you call building a career that requires zero emotional investment?"

"I call it survival," Jackie shot back. "Some of us can't afford to live in a fantasy world where love conquers all and good intentions pay the bills."

"And some of us can't afford to live in an emotional wasteland where success matters more than relationships."

But the real blow came at closing time, when Jovie showed them the day's receipts.

"We made money," Lauren said, sounding surprised.

"Not enough," Jackie said, studying the numbers.

"What do we do?" Lauren asked.

Jackie looked at her sister, at Melody quietly organizing the kitchen despite their chaos, at Jovie protecting Uncle Charlie Joe's legacy. She thought about the customers they'd disappointed, the opportunity they were wasting, the family they were destroying.

"I don't know," she said honestly. "But I can't keep fighting with you every day. One of us is going to have to give in, or we're both going to lose everything."

"I'm not giving in," Lauren said firmly.

"Neither am I."

Their eyes met over an expanse of unspoken wounds that seemed to have no end. Neither willing to compromise, yet neither willing to give up.

"Then we're screwed," Lauren said quietly.

"No. We just need to figure out how to work together, find the things we are each willing to compromise on and those we aren't. We also need to find out what Uncle Charlie Joe was hiding," Jackie said. "Because I'm starting to think this isn't just about real estate."

"Okay. What do you mean?"

"I mean someone's willing to commit crimes to get us off this property. The sabotage of the smoker and the text. We have the neighbor on one side and the developer on the other, both making veiled threats. That suggests there's something here worth more than land value." Jackie gestured toward the restaurant. "And whatever it is, Uncle Charlie Joe left us clues to find it."

"The safe," Melody said suddenly. "We need to examine everything in the safe."

"Tonight," Jackie agreed. "After we're sure we're alone."

But as they locked up the restaurant, Jackie couldn't shake the feeling that they weren't alone at all. Someone was watching, waiting, planning their next move.

Chapter Six

Overnight, the sisters made promises to themselves that they would try harder to be a team player. Deep down they wanted this to work, needed it to work for nearly the same reasons. Lauren for financial freedoms and Jackie to start over.

They were all exhausted, so they didn't make it to the office to check it out. The three of them collapsed immediately.

"We'll try for tonight," Jackie suggested over coffee the next morning.

Despite the rough day one, the second day went better, though Jackie's entire body ached from muscles she'd forgotten she had. Today they served thirty-one customers, including several who complimented the food and promised to bring friends.

They'd even shared a few laughs together and were more relaxed with each other. They hadn't fought and really tried to focus on their goal of making this place work.

Even more encouraging, Frank Kowalski had returned with his neighbor, Mrs. Claire Rigby, who ordered enough brisket and chicken to feed her entire book club. She would pick it up tomorrow. Jackie was glad they hadn't scared him off and got a new customer in the process.

"Word's spreading," Jovie said with satisfaction as they cleaned up after the lunch rush. "Nothing advertises a restaurant like happy customers."

Jackie bit her tongue wanting to point out that nobody had been happy yesterday. Instead, she tried to be optimistic and positive. It beat fighting and frowning.

Melody had spent the afternoon fine-tuning her optimization suggestions, creating detailed charts that showed customer flow patterns and peak ordering times. "If we adjust the menu layout and pre-portion certain sides, we could reduce average order time by eighteen percent," she announced.

"Eighteen percent?" Lauren asked. "That seems very specific."

"I timed every transaction," Melody said matter-of-factly. "Data doesn't lie."

Jackie was really learning to appreciate her niece's systematic approach more with each day. What she'd initially mistaken for obsessive behavior was actually incredibly valuable business analysis. Melody saw patterns that others missed and could optimize systems in ways that seemed almost magical.

She would have been a real asset in the corporate world, especially with a few of Jackie's more detailed cases. If she went back to her law practice, she'd have to consider consulting with Melody if she got stuck.

"We should talk about staffing," Jovie said, settling into a chair with a cup of coffee. "I can't do this alone much longer, and you three are still learning."

"What do you suggest?" Jackie asked.

"We need at least one more person for the kitchen and someone to help with front of house during busy periods." Jovie consulted her phone. "I know a few people who might be interested, but hiring means more expenses."

"How much more?" Lauren asked.

Jackie pulled out her notebook where she'd been tracking their finances. "Based on yesterday and today, we're averaging about four hundred dollars in revenue per day. Food costs are running about thirty percent, so that's roughly two-eighty profit before other expenses."

"That's not enough to hire anyone," Lauren said, deflated.

"Not yet," Jackie agreed. "But if we can build the customer base and maybe add some catering jobs, it could bring in enough."

"How are we going to add catering jobs when we barely have enough hands to run the restaurant?" Lauren asked.

"Well just like with Mrs. Rigby and her book club, we'll just take orders like that. We won't actually do service or deliveries ourselves, yet."

"That might work," Lauren said.

"Jovie," Jackie said, "I'd really like to see those financial records now. We need to understand our cash flow situation and if my numbers are in line with what has been done in the past."

"Tomorrow," Jovie said, stood and started wiping down the counter for the third time. "I promise. I just want to make sure everything's clear and accurate for you."

"How long does it take to organize basic financial records?" Jackie pressed.

"Well, there's the matter of... some irregularities I've been trying to resolve," Jovie admitted. "Nothing serious, just some discrepancies between what Charlie Joe recorded and what the bank statements show."

"What kind of discrepancies?" Lauren asked.

"Cash transactions mostly. Charlie Joe often helped people who couldn't afford to pay full price, but sometimes he didn't record those adjustments properly." Jovie's voice grew defensive. "And sometimes... well, sometimes bills had to be paid even when the register came up short."

"Are you saying you used restaurant money for other purposes?" Jackie asked directly.

"I'm saying I kept this place running when Charlie Joe wasn't able to manage the finances properly!" Jovie snapped, then immediately looked contrite. "I'm sorry. It's just been so stressful, trying to keep everything together while dealing with Emma's treatments."

"How much money are we talking about?" Melody asked quietly.

"A few thousand dollars over the past year," Jovie admitted. "All documented, all justified by business expenses or Charlie Joe's approval. I can show you the receipts."

"Okay, I look forward to seeing those," Jackie said.

Jovie looked from sister to sister unsure if she should share but knowing she needed to.

"There's something else," Jovie said quietly. "I got a phone call this morning from someone asking about Charlie Joe's 'business arrangements.'"

Jackie's attention sharpened. "What kind of business arrangements?"

"The caller wouldn't say. Just kept asking if Charlie Joe had any partners, any silent investors, anyone else involved in running the restaurant." Jovie frowned. "When I said no, he got pushy. Wanted to know about Charlie Joe's personal papers, his financial records."

"Did you recognize the voice?" Lauren asked.

"No, but it wasn't local. It was someone with a city accent, very smooth. Professional." Jovie's expression grew troubled. "He knew too much about the restaurant's history. Asked about specific equipment purchases from years ago, mentioned customers by name."

"Do you think it was someone from Kale's company?" Jackie asked.

"Could be but he didn't say so it would just be a guess," Jovie said.

Melody looked up from her charts. "Someone's been researching Uncle Charlie Joe very thoroughly."

"Too thoroughly," Jackie said grimly. "Between the threatening texts, the sabotage, and now this, someone's definitely trying to pressure us."

"But why?" Lauren asked. "If they just want to buy the property, why not make a legitimate offer and negotiate?"

"Technically, they have but we haven't been willing to hear them yet," Jackie pointed out. "But maybe it's not just about the property. Maybe Uncle Charlie Joe left something here that's worth more than real estate."

"Like what?" Jovie asked.

"I don't know yet," Jackie said. She planned to find out more tonight.

Jackie still had doubts about Jovie but felt maybe the woman was on their side. Jovie was in a hard position especially being left with the restaurant for the last few months by herself and business had taken a hit during that time as she just couldn't keep up. Plus, Jovie was dealing with a sick daughter. That had to weigh on her heavily.

However, Jackie still didn't want to fill her in on what the ladies planned to do that night. Not until she was sure Jovie was on their side.

As the evening rush started, they had a familiar face walk in.

"Hey, ladies," Harold Wilson said. "I haven't heard from y'all and wanted to see how you were settling in, and if you'd made a decision about the restaurant yet."

Lauren looked over at Jackie. Things hadn't been perfect, but it seemed they had made an unspoken agreement to keep the restaurant.

"Hi, Harold. Sorry, we've been busy learning the ropes," Jackie said. "I'm not sure we've made a final decision, but it is looking like we'll keep it in the family."

Lauren nodded. Jovie's face paled and she moved with almost robotic-like movements as she continued to fill orders.

"Well, okay, that's good. I'll let the investors know that you will not be selling," he said with a nod.

"You're still getting inquiries about selling?"

"Yes, very pushy people. They've gone up on their offer twice. We're talking … nearly two million," he whispered.

Jackie felt the room spin for a moment. Two million could really dig them both out of their financial holes. She looked over at Lauren who appeared to be calculating in her head.

The sisters locked eyes and had a silent conversation.

"Well, yes as we said, we believe we'll be keeping it in the family."

"Wonderful. I'll get all the paperwork together and send it over soon."

The lawyer ordered a rib plate to-go then nodded to them as he left.

One more piece of business done, Jackie thought. *Tonight, we find out what Charlie Joe was hiding.*

They waited until nearly ten PM to break out Uncle Charlie Joe's hidden documents, spreading everything across the restaurant's largest table like detectives working a case. The envelope marked "For My Family" sat unopened in the center, surrounded by photographs, papers, and the mysterious third key.

"Should we read the letter first?" Lauren asked, picking it up and checking the weight in her hand.

"Let's look at everything else first," Jackie suggested. "I want to understand the context before we hear Uncle Charlie Joe's explanation."

Melody had already begun organizing the photographs by date, her systematic approach revealing a pattern none of them had noticed before. "These aren't random pictures," she announced. "They tell a story, but it's not the complete story."

The earliest photos showed a much younger Uncle Charlie Joe in what appeared to be an office setting. He was wearing an expensive suit, confident smile, shaking hands with men in similar attire. He looked successful, polished, nothing like the humble pit boss they'd known him to be.

"He looks like a businessman," Lauren observed.

"He looks like you," Melody told Jackie. "Same posture, same expression when you're negotiating."

Jackie looked at her niece, then studied the picture carefully. She wasn't wrong.

"I guess the apple didn't fall far from the tree," Jackie said with a chuckle.

The next group of photos showed a transition period as Uncle Charlie Joe's suits became more casual, his smile more strained, and his eyes seemed to dim. In several pictures, he was cleaning out an office, boxing files, looking over his shoulder as if afraid of being watched.

"He was running from something," Lauren said quietly.

"Yes, but the bigger question, who took the pictures?" Jackie asked.

"And how did he get them?"

But the final set of photos showing his arrival in Prairie Rose seemed deliberately incomplete. There were pictures of him buying the land, building the restaurant, learning barbecue from Ezra Hutchins, but there were gaps. Missing months, missing relationships, missing explanations.

"It's like he edited his own history," Jackie observed. "Kept just enough to remember, but not enough to incriminate anyone."

Melody had moved on to the documents which included old bank statements, legal papers, and newspaper clippings. But these too seemed carefully curated.

"These are breadcrumbs," she said, holding up a bank statement with several entries blacked out. "He wanted us to find some information, but not all of it."

Jackie picked up a newspaper clipping with a headline that made her blood run cold: "Financial Adviser Questioned in Investment Fraud." But crucial details had been carefully cut away like dates, names, and specific amounts.

"He's protecting someone," Lauren realized. "Or protecting us from knowing too much."

"But protecting us from what?" Jackie asked.

Before anyone could answer, Melody's sharp intake of breath drew their attention. She was staring at her laptop screen, her face pale.

"I cross-referenced the partial information in these documents with online databases," she said quietly. "I found something Uncle Charlie Joe didn't want us to find easily."

"What?" Both sisters asked simultaneously.

"Richardson Financial Partners. Charles Joseph Wagner." Melody turned her laptop so they could see the screen. "But that's not the important part. The important part is that the case was never actually closed."

Jackie felt ice forming in her stomach. "What do you mean?"

"I mean Gerald Pemberton was convicted, but Charles Joseph Wagner was never officially cleared. He's still wanted for questioning." Melody's voice was very steady, very calm. "And according to this FBI database, the case was reactivated eight months ago."

"Eight months ago," Lauren repeated. "Right around the time Uncle Charlie Joe started getting those threatening phone calls."

"So, someone found him," Jackie said.

"Someone's been looking for him for thirty years," Melody corrected. "But eight months ago, they finally got close."

They sat in silence, absorbing the implications. Uncle Charlie Joe hadn't just been hiding from criminals. He'd been hiding from law enforcement too, and now they'd inherited not just his restaurant, but his legal problems.

"There's more," Melody said quietly. "The reactivation of the case wasn't random. It was triggered by new evidence. Evidence that suggests Wagner, Uncle Charlie Joe, may have been innocent all along."

"Then why didn't he come forward?" Lauren asked.

"That's a good question that I don't think we'll answer tonight."

Lauren nodded and shuffled through some of the documents while Melody continued searching on the computer.

Jackie watched them as she fought a yawn.

"Oh, don't start that," Lauren said through a yawn.

"Sorry. These early mornings and busy days," Jackie said.

"Yes. My body is so sore." Lauren laughed.

"We should lock this back up and call it a night."

"Sounds good. We aren't going to solve this tonight anyway."

With that, the trio locked everything back in the safe and headed to bed. Jackie kept thinking of the pictures and the redacted details. What was he hiding and if they started digging, were they safe?

Chapter Seven

The morning of their fourth day brought an unexpected visitor: a tall man in a khaki uniform with a badge that read "Sheriff Martinez, Prairie Rose County." He appeared at the front door just as they were finishing their morning prep, his presence both official and somehow reassuring.

"Morning, folks," he said, removing his hat to reveal graying temples and kind brown eyes. "I'm Sheriff Ray Martinez. Mind if I come in for a chat?"

Jackie felt her business instincts engage, but Lauren's stomach fluttered when their eyes met.

"Is there a problem, Sheriff?" Jackie asked.

"Nothing urgent," he said with a slight smile directed toward Lauren. "But I like to introduce myself to new business owners in my jurisdiction. Especially ones taking over establishments with as much history as this place."

Jovie emerged from the kitchen, wiping her hands on her apron. "Well, hey there, Ray Martinez," she said with obvious pleasure. "About time you stopped by. These are Charlie Joe's great-nieces, Jackie Prescott and Lauren Beniot, and Lauren's daughter Melody."

"The famous Rodriguez sisters," Sheriff Martinez said, shaking each of their hands in turn. "Charlie Joe mentioned you from time to time. Said you were both too stubborn for your own good, but he was proud of you anyway."

"We don't really go by Rodriguez any longer," Jackie said slightly annoyed by this stranger's assessment of them as stubborn.

"He talked about us?" Lauren asked, surprised.

"Not often, but when he did, it was always with affection." The Sheriff's expression grew more serious. "He also mentioned he was worried about some things, and said if anything ever happened to him, his family might need looking after."

"What kind of things was he worried about?" Jackie asked as her attitude changed from slightly annoyed to curiosity. Charlie Joe knew they might be in trouble.

Sheriff Martinez glanced around the dining room, taking in the photos and memorabilia. "Charlie Joe was a private man, but he'd been getting phone calls the last few months that bothered him. Strangers asking too many questions, people driving by the property at odd hours."

"Did he file any reports?" Jackie asked, her lawyer instincts engaging.

"Charlie Joe didn't trust authority much," Sheriff Martinez said with a rueful smile. "Can't say I blamed him. But he trusted me and asked me to keep an eye on the place. He said his family deserved to feel safe if they ever came home."

Melody, who had been quietly observing the conversation, suddenly spoke up. "Uncle Charlie Joe expected us to accept the inheritance terms and business."

"I think he hoped you would," the Sheriff agreed. "He believed strongly in family taking care of family."

"Have you noticed anything unusual lately?" Lauren asked. "Strange cars, unfamiliar people asking questions?"

Sheriff Martinez consulted a small notebook. "Had a complaint about suspicious activity near the old creek road three nights ago. Someone reported seeing vehicles parked back there with their lights off. By the time my deputy checked it out, they were gone."

Jackie and Lauren exchanged glances. Three nights ago was the day after they'd received the threatening text.

"Any other incidents?" Jackie asked.

"Few folks in town mentioned strangers asking about Charlie Joe's family, whether he had any relatives who might be coming around. Most people didn't know much to tell them, but it's got some of the older residents nervous."

"Nervous how?" Jovie asked.

"Prairie Rose is a small town. We notice when outsiders start asking too many questions about our people." Sheriff Martinez put his hat back on, tipping it in Lauren's direction. She would have missed it entirely if she hadn't been looking right at him. "I want you ladies to know that you're not alone here. This community looks after its own and Charlie Joe was one of us which makes you part of our community now too."

"We appreciate that," Jackie said sincerely.

"I also want you to know that my department takes threats seriously, whether they're made in person or through other means." His gaze was steady and knowing. "If you've received any communications that made you uncomfortable, I'd like to hear about them."

Jackie hesitated, then pulled out her phone and showed him the threatening text. Sheriff Martinez read it carefully, his expression growing darker.

"You should have reported this immediately," he said.

"We didn't think there was much you could do about anonymous texts," Lauren said.

"Maybe not about the texts themselves, but I can increase patrols in this area, and I can start building a case file." He photographed the messages with his own phone. "Mind if I ask what someone might want from you badly enough to threaten you?"

"We're still figuring that out," Jackie said honestly.

Sheriff Martinez studied her for a moment, clearly sensing there was more to the story. "Charlie Joe left you more than just a restaurant, didn't he?"

"What makes you say that?" Melody asked.

"Because in my experience, people don't threaten folks over barbecue recipes, no matter how good they are." His smile was gentle but perceptive. His gaze settled on Lauren. "Charlie Joe was a good man, but he had secrets. Most folks around here figured that out years ago."

"What kind of secrets?" Lauren asked.

"The kind a man keeps when his past is complicated." Sheriff Martinez leaned against the counter. "I've been a deputy here for fourteen years and only sheriff for about two months. In that time, Charlie Joe never once asked for a background check on an employee, never applied for any permits that required personal information, never did anything that might put his name in official records."

"That's not illegal," Jackie said.

"No, but it's unusual. Most business owners end up dealing with bureaucracy whether they want to or not." The Sheriff's expression grew thoughtful. "Charlie Joe managed to avoid it completely. That takes planning."

"Or experience," Melody said quietly.

"Exactly." Sheriff Martinez straightened up. "Look, I don't know what Charlie Joe was running from, and frankly, it wasn't my business as long as he wasn't hurting anyone. But if his past is catching up with his family, that is my business."

"What are you suggesting?" Jackie asked.

"I'm suggesting that if you find anything that explains why people are threatening you, you bring it to me immediately. Don't try to handle it yourselves." His voice carried the authority of someone used to being obeyed. "And I'm also suggesting you might want to stay together, especially at night."

"We're already doing that," Lauren said.

"Good. Keep doing it." Sheriff Martinez handed Lauren his business card. "My cell phone number's on there. Call me if anything else happens, day or night."

As he prepared to leave, he paused at the door. "One more thing. Charlie Joe asked me to give his family a message if they ever showed up. He said to tell you that the truth was more important than safety, but family was more important than either."

"What do you think he meant by that?" Lauren asked.

"I think he meant that whatever he was hiding, he hoped you'd have the courage to see it through. But not at the cost of losing each other." Sheriff Martinez touched the brim of his hat again as his eyes were on Lauren. The simple gaze caused her face to warm. "Take care of yourselves, ladies. And remember you're not alone in this."

After he left, the four women stood in contemplative silence.

"I like him," Melody announced finally.

"Why?" Jackie asked, curious about her niece's assessment.

"He asked questions without demanding answers. He offered help without taking control. And he understood that Uncle Charlie Joe was protecting us even after he died." Melody paused. "Those are indicators of trustworthiness."

"Plus, he's easy on the eyes," Jovie added with a grin.

"Jovie!" Lauren protested, but she was blushing.

"What? I'm old, not dead. You're single, and he kept looking at you like he'd noticed that fact."

Jackie studied her sister's reaction with interest. Lauren hadn't shown interest in anyone since Melody's father left, claiming she didn't have time for relationships. But the way she'd responded to Sheriff Martinez suggested otherwise.

"He was being professional," Lauren said primly.

"He was being interested," Jovie corrected. "There's a difference."

"Can we focus on the important things?" Jackie asked. "Like the fact that Sheriff Martinez basically confirmed that Uncle Charlie Joe was hiding from something, and that something is now threatening us?"

"He also confirmed that we have allies," Melody pointed out. "Law enforcement support is a significant tactical advantage."

"Tactical advantage?" Lauren asked.

"If we're going to uncover Uncle Charlie Joe's secrets, it's good to know we have someone in authority who's already predisposed to help us." Melody consulted her notebook. "Sheriff Martinez established trust, offered protection, and demonstrated understanding of complex family dynamics. He's a valuable resource."

"She's right," Jackie said. "Having him on our side could make all the difference."

"Assuming we can put all these pieces together," Lauren said.

"We will," Jackie said quietly. "Charlie Joe didn't go to all that trouble hiding documents, putting those specific photos together, and building safes for family recipes."

As they prepared for another day of serving customers and running the restaurant, Jackie couldn't shake the feeling that Sheriff Martinez's visit had been perfectly timed. Almost as if Uncle Charlie Joe had somehow arranged for them to meet the man who might help them survive whatever they were about to discover.

But that was impossible. Uncle Charlie Joe was dead, and the living had to find their own way through the maze of secrets he'd left behind.

Still, as Jackie watched Lauren stealing glances out the window in the direction Sheriff Martinez had gone, she smiled secretly.

My sister has a little crush, she thought.

After their lunch rush, they had another unexpected visitor. This time it was the town's doctor and the man who had signed off on their uncle's death certificate without an autopsy.

But the thing Jackie noticed immediately was that Dr. Michael Thorne appeared looking haggard and nervous in a way that immediately put her on alert.

"Hi, I'm Dr Michael Thorne," he said walking to the counter.

"Dr. Thorne. Nice to meet you," Lauren said, recognizing him from a couple of the pictures on the wall. "This is unexpected."

"I've been meaning to stop by," he said, taking a seat at one of the counter stools with the careful movements of someone trying to appear casual while feeling anything but. "Wanted to see how you ladies were settling in, offer any medical support you might need as new residents."

Jackie studied the doctor carefully. He was younger than she'd expected, probably in his early forties, with the kind of nervous energy that suggested he was carrying more stress than his small-town practice should generate.

"That's very thoughtful," she said, setting a coffee cup in front of him. "Though we're all pretty healthy."

"Good, good. That's... that's important." Dr. Thorne fidgeted with the coffee cup. "Charlie Joe always said family was important. Taking care of each other, I mean."

"You knew Uncle Charlie Joe well?" Lauren asked.

"Well, enough. He came in occasionally for minor things. Nothing serious, just... routine concerns." Dr. Thorne's voice grew quieter. "Though toward the end, he seemed more worried about things. Stress, you know. The kind of stress that can be hard on the heart."

"What kind of stress?" Melody asked, looking up from her inventory charts.

"Oh, the usual things that worry older folks. Financial concerns, health concerns, worry about family." Dr. Thorne glanced around the restaurant nervously. "Charlie Joe mentioned he was thinking about his legacy, what would happen to this place if something happened to him."

"When did he mention that?" Jackie asked.

"His last visit. Maybe three weeks before... before he passed." Dr. Thorne's hands tightened on the warm mug. "He asked me about heart attack symptoms, what the warning signs were, how quickly they could come on."

"That seems like an odd conversation," Lauren observed.

"I thought so too, at the time. But Charlie Joe said he'd been having chest pains, some shortness of breath, and he wanted to know if those were serious symptoms." Dr. Thorne's voice grew more strained. "I told him they could be, advised him to come back if they got worse, suggested he might want to consider stress reduction techniques."

"Did he seem worried about specific stressors?" Melody asked.

"He mentioned people asking questions about his past, strangers in town who seemed too interested in his business. Said it was making him nervous, affecting his sleep." Dr. Thorne looked directly at Jackie. "I advised him to talk to Sheriff Henderson if he felt threatened, but Charlie Joe said he didn't trust law enforcement to handle his situation appropriately."

"Why not?" Jackie asked.

"He didn't say specifically. Just that his problems were complicated and that involving the wrong people could make things worse." Dr. Thorne stood up abruptly. "I should get going. Just wanted to check on you ladies, make sure you knew medical care was available if you needed it."

"Dr. Thorne," Jackie said as he reached the door. "About Uncle Charlie Joe's death. You didn't feel an autopsy was necessary?"

The doctor went very still. "The symptoms were consistent with cardiac arrest. Given his age, his recent complaints, and the clear cause of death, an autopsy seemed... unnecessary. Expensive and traumatic for the family without providing useful information."

"Even though he died alone, with no witnesses?" Lauren asked.

"Cardiac events often happen when people are alone," Dr. Thorne said, but his voice lacked conviction. "Usually during sleep or periods of low activity when the heart is already stressed."

"But you're sure it was cardiac arrest?" Jackie asked.

Dr. Thorne hesitated for just a moment too long. "The symptoms were consistent with that diagnosis, yes."

After he left, the three women sat in uncomfortable silence.

"He's hiding something," Jackie said finally.

"He seemed genuinely troubled by Uncle Charlie Joe's death," Lauren observed. "Like he's been second-guessing his decisions."

"His body language suggested significant internal conflict," Melody added. "Classic signs of someone experiencing regret about a past decision."

"Well, whatever that was, he has guilt and a nervous energy about him," Jackie said. She'd learned to read body language and knew that that was a troubled man, and one they would need to watch.

Chapter Eight

The front door chimed. A woman in her seventies entered, moving with the careful precision of someone who'd learned not to trust her balance. She had silver hair pulled into a neat bun and sharp blue eyes that seemed to take in everything at once.

"Are you open?" she asked.

It was after their busy lunch time, and the restaurant was empty. They had learned to use this time to clean and restock to get ready for the next rush later in the day.

"Of course," Lauren said, standing up. "Please, sit anywhere you'd like."

The woman chose a table near the window and studied the menu carefully. When Lauren approached to take her order, she looked up with a smile that didn't quite reach her eyes.

"I'll have the sliced brisket sandwich with no sauce and extra pickles," she said. "And sweet tea. Charlie Joe always made the best sweet tea in the county."

"You knew Uncle Charlie Joe?" Lauren asked. Jovie left after their morning prep to accompany her daughter to an appointment, so Lauren couldn't look to the longtime employee for confirmation.

"Oh yes, dear. We were... old friends." The woman's smile became more genuine. "I'm Ruth Pemberton. I used to visit here quite regularly before Charlie Joe passed."

Jackie felt a chill run down her spine. Pemberton. As in Gerald Pemberton, the man from the newspaper articles they'd found in the safe. The only one convicted in the financial fraud case.

"Pemberton," she said carefully, approaching the table. "That's an unusual name around here."

"Is it?" Ruth asked innocently. "I suppose I never noticed. I'm not actually from Prairie Rose originally. I moved here about ten years ago to be closer to family."

Melody had stopped working on her charts and was studying Ruth with intense concentration. "You said you visited here regularly. What was your usual order?"

"Same as I ordered today. The brisket sandwich, no sauce, extra pickles," Ruth replied without hesitation. "Charlie Joe always remembered. Such a sweet man."

"If that is the same order, why did you study the menu so closely?"

"I always have a look in case I want a change, but I end up going back to my standard order. Creature of habit."

"I don't remember seeing you in any of the customer photos," Melody said.

Ruth's smile faltered slightly. "Oh, I never liked having my picture taken. I always asked Charlie Joe not to include me in those wall displays."

"I can understand that." Jackie smiled wanting to seem friendly enough to learn what the woman really wanted. "We have met a lot of people this week who knew him and shared stories."

"Oh, the stories I could tell," Ruth Pemberton said with a laugh.

"We'd love to hear one," Lauren said. "We're still learning about him ourselves."

She looked at the sisters standing in front of her. "You know his love of the community. Always willing to pitch in with meals or giving jobs to those in need."

Jackie's lawyer instincts were screaming that something was wrong. The woman knew too much about Uncle Charlie Joe's habits, but her answers felt rehearsed.

"Yes, we've heard that."

"We were all surprised to hear about his nieces taking over the restaurant," Ruth said.

"Great-nieces," Melody corrected. "And we're his only surviving family, according to the lawyer."

"Of course," Ruth said quickly. "I misspoke. It's wonderful that family is keeping the tradition alive."

"We were happy to take up what he started." Jackie said.

Lauren turned to grab the sandwich and sweet tea, bringing it over to the table. "Enjoy."

The sisters retreated back behind the counter to continue their afternoon duties, but they kept an eye on the stranger.

Ruth ate slowly, occasionally glancing around the dining room as if looking for something specific. When she finished, she left exact change plus a modest tip.

"Such nice girls," she said as she prepared to leave. "Charlie Joe would be so proud. I'm sure he left you *everything* you need to be successful."

After she was gone, the three women sat in uncomfortable silence.

"That was weird," Lauren said finally.

"That was reconnaissance," Jackie corrected. "She was fishing for information about what Uncle Charlie Joe left us."

"The name can't be a coincidence," Melody said. "Pemberton was Uncle Charlie Joe's co-worker from the financial firm."

"The articles didn't mention her," Jackie said.

"So, who is she?" Lauren asked.

"Could be a relative," Melody suggested. "Wife, daughter, sister."

"Either way, she knows more than she's letting on," Jackie said. "And I don't think we've seen the last of her."

As if summoned by Jackie's words, her phone buzzed with a text message. Unknown number again.

Ruth enjoyed her visit. Hope you enjoyed hers too. Some families have long memories.

Jackie showed the message to the others.

"They're watching us," Lauren said, fear creeping into her voice.

"And they're connected to Ruth Pemberton," Jackie said. "Which means this goes deeper than just wanting to buy our property."

"What do we do?" Lauren asked. "Let the Sheriff know?"

Jackie looked around the restaurant that Uncle Charlie Joe had built and loved. She thought about Frank Kowalski trusting them with his weekly routine, about Mrs. Rigby ordering food for her book club, about the community that depended on this place.

"Not yet. Instead, we figure out what Uncle Charlie Joe was really hiding," she said. "Because I have a feeling that until we do, the threats are only going to get worse."

"Tonight?" Lauren asked.

"Tonight," Jackie agreed. "We need to go back through all of those documents and photos. The answer has to be there."

They got back to work. There was always something to do around this place.

Jackie was checking inventory in the storage room when she heard Lauren's voice from the dining area, tense and uncomfortable.

"I told you, we're not interested in selling."

Jackie emerged to find Tom Whitfield standing just inside the front door, his hat in his hands but his posture aggressive. This time he wasn't on horseback. He'd driven a large pickup truck that he'd parked at an angle that blocked two other parking spaces.

"Tom," Jackie said coolly. "This is unexpected."

"Just being neighborly," Tom replied, but his eyes were hard. "Heard y'all had some threats?"

"How did you hear that?" Lauren asked.

"Word travels fast in small communities," Tom said with a slight smile.

"That seems like an odd and very specific thing to hear through the grapevine." Jackie's instincts were telling her this was not small-town gossip.

"Well people are talking about all the strangers in town. Those asking questions about the restaurant, about Charlie Joe, about his family." Tom's eyes narrowed on Jackie. "I've heard you've had customer complaints, equipment problems, and staff issues. That's a lot of challenges for folks who are new to the restaurant business."

"What staff issues?" Lauren asked.

"Well, there's Jovie's situation. Medical bills, financial pressure, access to your cash register and accounting systems." Tom's tone was casual, but his words were calculated to wound. "Sometimes people with money troubles make desperate choices, especially when they're working for employers who might not notice small discrepancies."

"Jovie is completely trustworthy," Jackie said firmly.

"Course she is. Just like Charlie Joe was completely safe, living alone out here with no security, no backup, nobody checking on him regularly." Tom's voice carried a note of mock sympathy. "Amazing how many accidents can happen to isolated folks who don't have strong community connections."

"Charlie Joe died of natural causes," Lauren said.

"So they say," Tom replied. "But natural causes can be hard to distinguish from other kinds of causes when nobody's looking too closely. Especially when the deceased was known to have enemies."

"What enemies?" Melody asked.

"Business enemies. People who didn't appreciate Charlie Joe's... unconventional approach to land use and community relations." Tom put his hat back on. "Of course, that's all in the past now. The important thing is making sure his successors don't repeat his mistakes."

"What kind of mistakes?" Jackie asked.

"The mistake of thinking you can ignore local customs and established relationships. The mistake of believing that legal ownership matters more than community harmony." Tom moved toward the door, then paused. "The mistake of assuming that isolation provides security instead of vulnerability."

After he left, the three women stood in uncomfortable silence.

"That felt like a threat," Lauren said finally.

"That was definitely a threat," Jackie agreed. "Multiple threats, actually."

"He knows about Jovie's financial situation," Melody observed. "That suggests he's been investigating our business affairs, possibly talking to our suppliers or customers."

"Or he's been watching us more closely than we realized," Jackie said grimly.

As they stood there, a dark car pulled to the side of the road. Not quite in the parking lot but obviously angled to look at them. A chill ran through Jackie.

"Who is that?"

"I can't tell."

A man stepped out looking right at them through the window. It was Harrison Kale. A slow smile crept across his face before he climbed back into the car, turning back the way he had just come from.

"Okay, that's strange, right?" Lauren asked.

"Very strange. It was like he wanted us to see him."

As they locked up the restaurant, none of them noticed the car parked at the edge of the property, or the telephoto lens aimed at the building. But they all felt the weight of invisible eyes watching their every move.

The restaurant had been closed for two hours, but none of them could sleep. They sat in the apartment's small living room, the weight of Ruth Pemberton's visit and the escalating threats pressing down on them like a physical presence.

"I keep thinking about what she said," Lauren murmured, curled up on one end of the couch with a cup of chamomile tea. "About Charlie Joe leaving us everything we need to be successful. Like she knew there was more than just the restaurant."

Jackie was at the kitchen table, surrounded by legal pads covered with notes and theories. Plus, all the photos from the safe. Melody had put them in chronological order for her.

"She definitely knew more than she was letting on. The question is whether she's working with whoever's been threatening us, or if she has her own agenda."

"Could be both," Melody said from her spot on the floor, where she'd spread out all their financial records and timeline of events. "Multiple parties with different but overlapping interests in Uncle Charlie Joe's legacy."

Outside, the wind picked up, rattling the old windows and making the building creak. Jackie found the sounds oddly comforting. The restaurant felt solid, permanent, like something that had weathered many storms and would weather many more.

"Can I ask you something?" Lauren said suddenly, looking at Jackie. "Before Dad and Mom split up, do you remember what we were like together?"

Jackie set down her pen, surprised by the question. "What do you mean?"

"I mean, do you remember being friends? Before we had to choose sides?"

Jackie was quiet for a moment, searching through memories that felt ancient. "I remember that summer when you broke your arm," she said finally. "You were maybe eight? I convinced you to try to jump from the garage roof to the oak tree."

"You had made it look easy, but when I did it, I missed and fell into Mom's flower bed." Lauren smiled despite herself. "You carried me into the house, told them it was your fault, took the punishment."

"You were crying so hard I thought you'd broken more than just your arm."

"I was scared Mom would be mad at me for ruining her roses. You knew that, so you took the blame." Lauren's voice grew softer. "When did we stop protecting each other like that?"

"When protecting each other meant choosing between our parents," Jackie said. "When we realized that taking care of each other might mean hurting the parent we'd chosen to support. I think... I think I carried that fear into my own parenting. I was so afraid of putting my sons in the middle of anything that I taught them to be completely self-sufficient instead."

"Is that why Alec and Caden are so distant?" Lauren asked gently.

Jackie nodded. "I raised them to never need anyone, never depend on family for emotional support. I thought I was making them strong. Turns out I was just making them... unreachable."

"They're not unreachable," Melody said from her spot on the floor. "They're just following the relationship model you taught them. Emotional distance as self-protection."

"Great," Jackie said with a bitter laugh. "So, I broke my relationship with my sister and then used that broken model to break my relationships with my sons too."

"Recognition of patterns is the first step toward changing them," Melody observed. "You're here now, choosing family connection over self-protection. That's different behavior."

Jackie paused, thinking about her niece's words. She had no words, no reply. Melody wasn't wrong.

"That's messed up," Melody observed without looking up from her papers. "Children shouldn't have to choose between their parents or between each other."

"No, they shouldn't," Jackie agreed. "But we did. And then we spent over thirty-five years being angry about choices we made when we were too young to understand what we were choosing."

Lauren pulled her knees up to her chest. "I've been thinking about that a lot, especially since we've been here. About how Melody never had to make those kinds of choices because her father just... left. No custody battles, no taking sides, just gone."

"Which was better in some ways," Melody said pragmatically. "Abandonment is cleaner than forced loyalty conflicts. Less ongoing psychological damage."

"Melody!" Lauren protested.

"What? It's true. My father left when I was two. I have no memory of family conflict involving him. You and Jackie spent most of your childhoods navigating divided loyalties. My situation was simpler."

Jackie studied her niece again. Each day Melody surprised her with her honest, unapologetic observations on life. "You know, you're probably right. We never thought about it that way."

"Most people don't," Melody said. "They assume that having an absent parent is worse than having divorced parents who put their children in the middle. But research suggests that high-conflict divorced families cause more long-term psychological harm than single-parent families."

"Where did you learn all this?" Lauren asked.

"Therapy. Books. Online research." Melody finally looked up from her papers. "I wanted to understand why my family was broken, so I studied family systems theory."

"And what did you conclude?" Jackie asked.

"That families break for lots of reasons, but they usually stay broken because people are too proud or too scared to do the work required to fix them." Melody's gaze moved between Jackie and Lauren. "Also, children often carry their parents' emotional burdens long into adulthood."

The observation hung in the air like a challenge.

"So, what are we carrying?" Lauren asked quietly.

"Grandpa's sense of abandonment," Melody said matter-of-factly. "Grandma's sense of betrayal. Their inability to forgive each other became your inability to forgive each other."

Jackie felt exposed, like Melody had shined a light into corners of her psyche she'd kept carefully dark. "That's... probably accurate."

"Definitely accurate," Lauren agreed. "I spent years being angry at you for 'abandoning Dad' because that's how Dad felt about Mom leaving. And you spent years being angry at me for 'enabling Dad's victim mentality' because that's how Mom felt about Dad's behavior during the divorce."

"We became proxies for their fight," Jackie realized.

"And then you inherited their inability to resolve conflict constructively," Melody added. "Which is why Uncle Charlie Joe had to manipulate you into working together. He knew you'd never choose to do it voluntarily."

When they finally went to sleep later, Lauren lay in bed listening to the crickets outside and Melody's even breathing. She wondered if tonight's revelation would end their fighting. She wasn't sure, but so glad they had a nice evening.

Chapter Nine

The sixth morning brought a challenge that Lauren never saw coming, though looking back, she should have recognized the warning signs building for days.

The first indication something was wrong came at 3 AM when Lauren woke to find Melody's bed empty. She found her daughter in the bathroom, sitting fully clothed in the empty bathtub, rocking back and forth with her hands pressed tightly over her ears.

"Melody?" Lauren whispered, but her daughter didn't respond. The rhythmic tapping that usually calmed her had become frantic scratching at her jeans, and her breathing was rapid and shallow.

Lauren knew better than to touch her when she was like this. Instead, she sat quietly on the bathroom floor, waiting and hoping this wouldn't escalate into a full meltdown. Melody had been doing so well, as long as they'd stuck to their schedule, so there hadn't been a meltdown in nearly a year.

But by 4:30, when Jackie's alarm went off, Melody was curled in a tight ball but now on her bed, still fully dressed from the day before, making a low humming sound that Lauren recognized as her daughter's attempt to block out overwhelming stimuli.

"She's been like this for hours," Lauren explained quietly to Jackie outside the bedroom door. "Too much change, too much stress, too many new routines all at once. I should have seen it coming."

Jackie peered into the room where Melody was now covering her head with a pillow, her whole body tense with distress. "What usually helps?"

"Time. Quiet. Predictability." Lauren's voice was strained with worry and guilt. "Things we don't exactly have when we need to open a restaurant in thirty minutes."

That's when the real meltdown began.

The sound of Jovie's truck pulling up outside was like a match to kindling. Melody shot upright in bed, her face contorted with panic and frustration.

"NO!" The word came out as a raw scream. "No, no, no, I can't! Everything is wrong, everything is too much, too loud, too different!"

She began hitting her temples with her fists, the self-soothing behavior that terrified Lauren more than anything else. "Make it stop, make it all stop! I can't think, I can't breathe, everything is WRONG!"

"Melody, honey. " Lauren stepped forward, but Melody scrambled backward against the headboard.

"Don't touch me! Don't look at me! I can't ... I can't do this anymore!" Tears were streaming down her face now, her voice breaking with exhaustion. "Every day something new, every day more people, more noise, more decisions. I can't make my brain work right here!"

Jackie stood frozen in the doorway, watching her niece fall apart with a kind of helpless horror. This wasn't the calm, analytical young woman who'd been optimizing their restaurant operations. This was someone in genuine emotional and sensory crisis.

"I'm supposed to be helping," Melody sobbed, pulling at her hair. "I'm supposed to be good at organizing things, but I can't organize my own thoughts. I can't make the feelings stop or the noise in my head quiet down!"

"What feelings?" Lauren asked gently, keeping her distance but staying calm. "Can you tell me what you're feeling right now?"

"Everything! All at once!" Melody's voice cracked. "Scared that you and Jackie will start fighting again. Angry that people keep staring at me like I'm broken. Sad that Uncle Charlie Joe is dead and I never got to meet him. Overwhelmed because there are too many textures and smells and sounds and I can't filter them out anymore!"

She threw the pillow across the room with surprising force. "And I'm mad at myself for falling apart when you need me to be strong! I know you're depending on me, and I know the restaurant needs me, but I can't ... I just can't."

The words dissolved into incoherent sobs as Melody curled up again, her whole body shaking.

Jackie felt her own eyes fill with tears. She'd been so focused on Melody's helpful contributions that she'd missed the signs of someone pushed beyond their limits. "Melody, we're not depending on you to hold everything together. That's not your job."

"Yes, it is!" Melody's voice was muffled but fierce. "If I'm not useful, if I'm not helping solve problems, then I'm just... I'm just the difficult one. The one who needs accommodations and special treatment and —"

"Stop," Lauren said firmly, moving closer despite Melody's earlier protest. "You are not difficult. You are not a burden. You are my daughter, and you're struggling, and that's okay."

"But the restaurant ..."

"Will survive one day without your optimization charts," Jackie said, surprising herself with how certain she sounded. "We'll figure it out. We always do."

Melody looked up at them with red, swollen eyes. "But what if I can't get better? What if I can't handle this life we're building? What if I ruin everything for you?"

The raw vulnerability in her voice broke something open in Jackie's chest. She sat down on the edge of the bed, careful to maintain distance but close enough to be present.

"Melody, a week ago your mom and I couldn't be in the same room for twenty minutes without screaming at each other. We've all been learning how to do this. Nobody expects you to be perfect at it, especially after just a week."

"But you need me to be functional," Melody whispered.

"We need you to be honest," Lauren corrected. "When you're overwhelmed, when you need breaks, when the sensory stuff gets to be too much. We can't help if we don't know."

"I didn't want to be another problem to solve."

"You're not a problem," Jackie said. "You're family. And family takes care of each other when things get hard."

Melody was quiet for several long minutes, her breathing gradually slowing. Finally, she looked up at them with exhausted but clearer eyes.

"I think I need today to be very quiet and very predictable," she said in a small voice.

"Then that's what today will be," Lauren said immediately.

"But Jovie —"

"Can handle the morning prep with us," Jackie said. "And if we need to adjust how we do things to make them work better for you, then that's what we do. The restaurant serves us, not the other way around."

"Really?"

"Really," both sisters said simultaneously.

Melody managed a weak smile. "Could we... could we maybe have the same breakfast we had yesterday? And sit in the same spots? And maybe not change anything else today?"

"Absolutely," Lauren said. "And tomorrow, if you're feeling better, we can talk about what changes would help you feel more stable here."

"Like what?" Melody asked, seeming to brighten slightly at the prospect of problem-solving.

"Like maybe a quiet space you can retreat to when things get overwhelming," Jackie suggested. "Or a way to signal when you need breaks without having to explain everything."

"And maybe a more predictable schedule," Lauren added. "So you know what to expect each day."

"Those sound like good accommodations," Melody said, using the word without shame for the first time. "Not special treatment. Just... modifications that help me function better."

"Exactly," Jackie said. "The same way we modified our workflow to be more efficient. This is just optimizing for different variables."

Melody actually laughed at that, though it was still shaky. "You're getting better at speaking my language."

"I'm learning," Jackie said. "We all are."

As they helped Melody get ready for a quieter version of their usual morning routine, Jackie realized that seeing her niece's vulnerability had made her more precious, not less. The breakdown hadn't revealed weakness, it had revealed the tremendous effort Melody had been putting into adapting to their new life.

"Next time," Jackie said as they headed downstairs, "tell us before it gets this bad. We're tougher than we look. We can handle adjusting things for you."

"And next time," Lauren added, "remember that taking care of yourself isn't selfish. It's how you take care of the family."

Melody nodded, looking more like herself as they entered the familiar environment of the restaurant kitchen. "Can I still do the inventory later? When I'm feeling more stable?"

"Only if you want to," Jackie said. "And only if it feels good instead of stressful."

"It usually feels good," Melody admitted. "Numbers are soothing when everything else feels chaotic."

"Then numbers it is," Lauren said, kissing her daughter's forehead. "But first, breakfast. Same as yesterday."

As they settled into their modified routine, Jackie marveled at how much she'd learned about her niece and about family in the span of one difficult morning. Melody's meltdown hadn't been a setback. It had been an honest expression of feeling overwhelmed that had ultimately brought them closer together.

And that, she thought as she watched Melody gradually relax into the predictable rhythm of their morning prep, was exactly the kind of authentic family relationship Uncle Charlie Joe had been hoping they'd build.

Chapter Ten

By the seventh day, the alarm at 4:30 AM was becoming easier to bear, but Jackie's muscles still protested as she rolled out of bed. After days of prepping, her hands were permanently stained with spice rub despite multiple washings.

"Coffee's ready," Melody announced from her usual spot at the table, surrounded by what appeared to be architectural drawings. At least she was out of bed today. "I've been designing an improved workflow pattern for the kitchen."

"Of course you have," Jackie said fondly. "How are you feeling today?"

"Rested," Melody said with her matter-of-fact tone.

Jackie smiled.

Lauren emerged from the bedroom looking more rested than she had in days. She headed for the coffee and then the three headed downstairs to meet Jovie.

"What's the lesson plan today, Chef Jovie?"

Jovie arrived even earlier than usual with her arms full of grocery bags and a determined expression. "Now that you've all learned the basics, it's time you learn the difference between good barbecue and great barbecue," she announced. "And why Charlie Joe's was great, even better than Ezra's."

The next hour was a masterclass in meat selection. Jovie led them through examining briskets like a sommelier evaluating wine as they checked marbling, thickness, and the way fat distributed through the muscle.

"This one," Jackie said, holding up a cut that looked identical to all the others.

"Why?" Jovie asked.

"Because... it looks good?"

"That's not analysis, that's hoping." Jovie picked up another brisket. "Look at the grain of the meat, the consistency of the fat cap, the flexibility when you bend it slightly."

Jackie tried again, this time actually studying the meat instead of guessing. "This one has more even marbling?"

"Better. Lauren, your turn."

Lauren proved to have an intuitive understanding of meat selection that surprised everyone, including herself. "This one feels right," she said, hefting a particularly thick cut. "The fat isn't too hard, and the color is consistent throughout."

"Exactly right," Jovie said with approval. "You've got natural instincts for this."

"I do?" Lauren looked pleased and surprised.

"Some people can learn technique, but you can't teach instinct." Jovie began demonstrating the trimming process. "Your sister's got good analytical skills, but you've got the feel for it."

Jackie felt a flash of something that might have been jealousy, then pushed it aside. Lauren deserved to be good at something, to feel confident and capable. Jackie had spent most of her adult life being the successful one; it was Lauren's turn to shine.

The trimming lesson proved to be Jackie's nemesis. Her knife work was precise but slow, each cut carefully calculated. Lauren's was faster and somehow more natural, following the contours of the meat with an ease that Jovie praised.

"You're thinking too much," Jovie told Jackie. "Trust your hands."

"My hands don't know what they're doing," Jackie replied, frustrated by her fourth attempt at achieving the perfect fat cap thickness.

"They will. Muscle memory takes time." Jovie moved to help Melody, who had been observing the process with intense focus. "Want to try?"

"I'll watch for now," Melody said. "I'm developing a theoretical framework before attempting practical application."

"She's memorizing your technique," Lauren translated. "When she's ready to try, she'll probably be perfect on the first attempt."

"Perfectionism runs in your family," Jovie observed. "Charlie Joe was the same way. Drove himself crazy trying to get every detail exactly right."

The fire management lesson went better for Jackie. The systematic approach to temperature control appealed to her methodical nature. She learned to read the smoke. White meant too much moisture, black meant too hot, the perfect thin blue smoke meant everything was working correctly.

"Fire is chemistry," Jovie explained, watching Jackie adjust the air vents with growing confidence. "Combustion rates, heat transfer, oxidation. It's all science."

"I can work with science," Jackie said, successfully maintaining 235 degrees for twenty minutes straight.

"Science with art," Jovie corrected. "You can know all the theory in the world, but every piece of wood burns differently, every day has different humidity, every cut of meat has its own personality."

By mid-morning, they had half a dozen briskets smoking and all the other meats, and were ready for the lunch prep. This was where Melody finally stepped forward, having absorbed hours of observation into what appeared to be a comprehensive understanding of restaurant operations.

"The vegetable prep station is inefficiently organized," she announced, surveying the kitchen. "Tools are stored by type rather than by frequency of use. Cutting boards are stacked rather than hung for easy access. The workflow creates unnecessary steps."

"Show me," Jovie said.

What followed was thirty minutes of Melody reorganizing the prep area with the precision of a military operation. She moved equipment, rearranged storage, and created what she called "task-specific zones" that would minimize movement and maximize efficiency.

"Try making coleslaw now," she told Jackie.

Jackie was amazed at the difference. Everything she needed was within arm's reach, the cutting board was at the perfect height, and the process that had taken her twenty minutes yesterday now took twelve.

"That's incredible," Lauren said, trying the new setup herself. "How did we not see this sooner?"

"It's logical," Melody replied. "Uncle Charlie Joe's system worked, but it evolved organically over thirty years. I optimized it based on current usage patterns. It keeps the spirit of his original process of hand shredding but speeds it to be almost as efficient as using a food processor."

Jackie remembered the intense fight from days ago. Melody clearly had too, and in her usual way, had found a solution.

Their first real test came at 11:30 when the early lunch crowd began arriving. Jackie found herself taking orders from people who knew exactly what they wanted and had been coming here longer than she'd been alive.

"The usual, Frank?" she asked Frank Kowalski.

"You remember," he said with a smile that warmed her more than she'd expected. "Chopped brisket sandwich, sweet tea."

"Coming right up."

But it wasn't coming right up. With the changes they'd made today, Lauren was still learning to portion sides consistently, Jackie fumbled with the cash register that seemed to have been designed by someone who hated both technology and human fingers, and Melody was trying to help by calling out efficiency suggestions that nobody had time to implement.

"Order up!" Jovie called from the kitchen window, but Jackie was three customers behind on drinks and couldn't get to the pickup window.

"I've got it," a voice said behind her. A middle-aged woman with dark hair with streaks of steel-gray mixed in and kind eyes stepped behind the counter and began assembling orders with practiced ease. "I'm Maria Santos. I used to help Charlie Joe during busy periods."

"Thank you," Jackie said gratefully, finally catching up on beverages.

"Mind if I pitch in today?" Maria asked. "I miss this place, and you girls look like you could use an extra pair of hands."

"We'd love the help," Lauren called from where she was frantically spooning potato salad.

The next hour passed in a blur of sandwiches, sides, and sweet tea. With Maria's help, they managed to serve forty-three customers without any major disasters. When the rush finally ended, Jackie collapsed into a chair with profound respect for anyone who worked in food service.

"How do you do this every day? And how did you do this alone?" she asked Jovie. It had been their busiest day thus far as word spread about the restaurant's new owners.

"You build up to it. Plus, you get better at reading the rhythm." Jovie counted the lunch receipts with satisfaction. "Today was better than yesterday. Tomorrow will be better than today."

"Will you come back?" Lauren asked Maria.

"If you'll have me," Maria said. "Charlie Joe gave, not only me a job when I needed it, but also gave my son his first job here when no one else would hire a kid with a juvenile record. This place means something to my family."

"We can't pay much yet, but we'd love to have you."

"I don't need much. I just love the work and adult conversations."

"Great. We'll see you tomorrow."

As Maria left, promising to return the next day, Melody approached with her notebook full of observations.

"The changes we made this morning were good, but I've identified seventeen areas for improvement," she announced. "And also, twelve things we're doing very well."

"What are we doing well?" Lauren asked.

"Food quality is excellent. Customer interaction is genuine and warm. The atmosphere feels authentic." Melody consulted her notes. "People don't just come here for food. They come for community. That's Uncle Charlie Joe's real legacy."

"What are the seventeen improvements?" she asked.

"Would you like them prioritized by impact or by ease of implementation?"

"Both," Jackie and Lauren said simultaneously, then looked at each other and laughed.

The afternoon was spent implementing Melody's latest suggestions. They reorganized the front counter for better customer flow, created a system for tracking special orders, and established what Melody called "crisis protocols" for handling rush periods.

By closing time, Jackie felt like she'd run a marathon, but also like she'd accomplished something important. Her hands were raw from handling hot plates, her feet ached from standing all day, and she'd probably gained three pounds from sampling Jovie's cooking.

"Same time tomorrow?" Jovie asked as she cleaned the last of the equipment.

"Absolutely," Jackie said. "We'd talked about hiring employees, but we never got back to discussing it. Maybe now we should talk about hiring Maria permanently. I know we offered her at least one more day."

"And maybe one more person for busy periods," Lauren added.

"Revenue projections support modest staff expansion," Melody agreed, showing them her detailed financial analysis. "Current growth trajectory indicates we'll need additional help within two weeks."

"So, we all agree?"

"Yes."

"It would also be great if I could see those books, Jovie." Jackie looked at her.

Jovie paled. "I left them at home. I'll bring them tomorrow."

"Okay, tomorrow."

Jovie nodded.

As they locked up and headed upstairs, Jackie realized something had changed. Not just in their understanding of the restaurant business, but in her understanding of her family.

Lauren had natural talents that Jackie had never recognized. Melody's systematic approach wasn't just helpful. It was transformative. And Jackie herself had capabilities she'd never tested.

"You know what?" she said as they climbed the stairs. "I think we're actually going to be good at this."

"You sound surprised," Lauren said.

"I am surprised." She laughed. "Just days ago, I didn't know the difference between a brisket and a beef roast. Today I maintained fire temperature for six hours straight."

"Tomorrow you'll be even better," Melody said matter-of-factly. "Skill acquisition follows predictable patterns. We're all improving rapidly."

"Plus," Lauren added with a grin, "Jovie and Maria both said we have good instincts. I'm choosing to believe them."

"And we didn't get any threats or have any random craziness."

"True!"

As Jackie settled into bed that night, she realized she was looking forward to tomorrow. Not just because they were getting better at running the restaurant, but because she was getting better at being part of this family.

Neither of those things she'd thought she would ever do, but here it was her life now.

Chapter Eleven

The next day, Maria arrived at 9 am to assist with prep and the lunch rush.

"I've created a workflow that will show how the stations will run with an extra person," Melody said.

Jackie took the paper from her, studying it. "Wow, this is great. I think it'll work perfectly to incorporate another employee."

She passed it to Maria.

"This is impressive," she said reviewing it. She nodded. "I can follow this."

With that they all got to work with prepping. Maria stepped right in, following each recipe with practiced precision that only came from years of doing the work.

"How often did you work for Charlie Joe?" Jackie asked.

"Oh, off and on for years. When my children were young, I could work here during the day while they were at school then be home when they were out."

"That is a consistent schedule," Melody observed.

"It was. Your great-uncle was extremely generous and understood what it took to help people," she said with a sigh. "He was one of the good ones. I really miss him."

"We keep hearing that about him. I hate that we didn't get to know him better," Jackie said.

"What did happen? He never said, and spoke about you all as if he still had a relationship with you all," Maria said.

The sisters looked at each other.

"We really aren't sure. He is our grandmother's youngest brother. There was an eighteen- or nineteen-year difference between them. They were never close, but he would be at holidays sometimes," Jackie said, then looked at Lauren. "In fact, our mother is just a few years younger than him. They grew up almost like siblings."

"Yes, I remember he always brought us candy and gave us each a dollar when he'd see us. But then one day nobody talked about him any longer. He just ... disappeared."

"That must be when he made it here," Jovie said.

"Must be. I think Mom talked to him from time to time, since they grew up together, but we never really saw him again."

An uncomfortable silence sat around them. They continued prepping without another word for several long minutes.

They'd learned so much about their great-uncle this past week, so to think that they would never have a chance to truly get to know him was sad. Lauren looked over at Jackie. They smiled weakly at each other.

Here was their chance to repair their relationship with each other. Would they blow it?

They didn't have time to think about that now, as they had to open for the day, but the energy in the restaurant had shifted to one of mourning and regret.

Jackie tried to smile as she took customer orders, but her heart wasn't in it. When she'd caught Lauren's eye, her own feelings seemed to be reflected in them.

The lunch rush had been steady but manageable with Maria's help.

"Thank you so much for being here," Lauren said to Maria as they scooped coleslaw and potato salad to serve the last of the customers.

"My pleasure."

As the last lunch customer left and Maria said goodbye for the day, they began cleaning up, and Jackie pulled out a notebook she'd been scribbling in all morning.

"I've been thinking about some improvements we could make," Jackie said, spreading her notes across the counter. "Seeing how smoothly today went made me realize we need to modernize if we want to really succeed."

Jovie looked up from where she was restocking napkin dispensers. "Smoothly? Today went well because of Melody's new system and Maria knowing the ropes."

"Right, but I'm talking about bigger changes," Jackie continued. "That grill is ancient. We need a proper prep station with more counter space. Maybe even update the POS system."

"Jackie, slow down." Lauren set down her rag. "Melody's been working on improvements all week. The workflow system, the new inventory tracking, reorganizing the walk-in cooler..."

Melody looked up from her own notebook where she'd been updating the day's numbers. "The efficiency improvements are already showing results. We served twelve percent more customers today with the same labor hours."

"That's great, but we're thinking too small," Jackie said dismissively. "We need equipment upgrades, marketing strategies —"

"Too small?" Lauren's voice had an edge. "Melody's system is what made today work, the last several days, in fact. And Jovie's been keeping this place running practically single-handed. Plus, Maria was a huge help today."

Jovie nodded. "Charlie Joe and I managed just fine with what we had. Sometimes the old ways work."

"That's exactly my point," Jackie said. "We can't just maintain the status quo. Uncle Charlie Joe barely scraped by, and we need to think bigger if we want to actually succeed."

The room went quiet.

"Uncle Charlie Joe did just fine," Lauren said slowly. "And maybe you should pay attention to the improvements that are already happening before you dismiss everything."

"I'm not dismissing anything. I'm just saying we need real investment: new equipment, professional marketing, maybe expand the menu perhaps."

"Expand the menu?" Jovie laughed. "We can barely manage what we have."

Jackie's face flushed. "Look, I appreciate everyone's efforts, but I have actual business experience. I know what it takes to scale a restaurant operation."

"Scale?" Lauren stepped closer. "This isn't some franchise opportunity, Jackie. And Melody's improvements aren't just 'efforts'. They're working."

"I never said they weren't working, but —"

"But what? They're not impressive enough for you?" Lauren's voice was getting louder. "Melody spent hours creating systems that actually solved our problems, and you walk in here with a notebook full of expensive ideas like none of that matters."

Melody looked between her mother and aunt, then quietly said, "the current improvements have increased efficiency without additional overhead costs."

"See?" Lauren gestured toward her daughter. "Real solutions, not just throwing money at problems."

"I understand business fundamentals, Lauren. Something you clearly don't if you think small tweaks are going to be enough, especially if we want to hire more employees."

The silence that followed was deafening. Jovie set down the napkins and backed toward the kitchen. Melody clutched her pen tighter.

"There it is," Lauren said quietly. "The real Jackie. I wondered how long it would take for you to remind us all how much smarter you think you are than the rest of us."

"That's not what I —"

"It's exactly what you meant." Lauren untied her apron with shaking hands. "You just dismissed everything Melody's accomplished, everything Jovie's done to keep this place alive, like it's all worthless because it wasn't your idea."

"Lauren, that's not —"

"You know what? Maybe you should run this place by yourself. Make all your big improvements. Turn it into whatever corporate vision you have in mind."

"Mom," Melody said softly, but Lauren was already heading for the front door.

"I need some air. Melody, you did amazing work today. Don't let anyone tell you otherwise."

The door slammed behind her, leaving Jackie standing in the sudden quiet, realizing she'd just alienated not only Lauren, but the two people who'd been making the restaurant actually work.

"Melody, you know I appreciate all your efforts, right?" Jackie pleaded.

"I do."

"I was just trying to add some value also."

Melody didn't speak, just began tapping her fingers in the usual soothing pattern. Jackie knew she had crossed a line but thought her approach would work to increase business. She had just gone about it the wrong way.

Perhaps once everyone calmed down, they could discuss further. She got back to cleaning while Lauren cooled off and Melody calmed herself.

It was another ten minutes before Lauren returned but didn't speak. She just began taking out the trash.

That's when Jovie burst through the kitchen door announcing the second sabotage attempt, but they were too emotionally drained to care much about the overheated smoker. They had bigger problems than whoever was trying to run them off.

But reluctantly they followed Jovie outside to find the temperature gauge reading nearly 400 degrees. The firebox had been stuffed with fresh wood, creating an inferno that threatened to ruin the brisket.

"Can we save it?" Lauren asked anxiously.

Jovie was already pulling wood from the firebox with heavy gloves. "Maybe. But this was no accident. Someone added this wood in the last thirty minutes."

Jackie looked toward the tree line where they'd seen the saboteur that first day. "Someone's trying to make sure we fail," Jackie said. "And they're getting bolder."

They managed to save most of the brisket, though it would be drier than Uncle Charlie Joe's standards. As the afternoon wore on, Jackie found herself checking the windows constantly, waiting for the next attack.

There was no sign of anyone. Not at the road where they'd seen Harrison Kale and not from the fence line where Tom Whitfield seemed to be an almost ever presence. It was enough to keep Jackie on edge though.

Jackie had been putting off the financial review long enough. Despite the chaos, arguing and sabotage that had taken place that day, she knew she had to address her suspicion with Lauren and Melody.

That evening, after they'd locked up and Jovie had left for the day, she said to Lauren and Melody, "We need to talk about Jovie."

"What about her?" Lauren asked, though her tone suggested she'd been having her own concerns.

"She said she'd have the books to us today, but nothing. No mention of them. I didn't bring it up either because I wanted to give her a chance."

"We had a few other things going on today."

Jackie looked at her. "You're right, and I'm sorry for my part."

"Me too."

"But I just keep thinking about the financial irregularities. The way she's been evasive about the books. Her daughter's medical bills." Jackie pulled out her own notebook where she'd been tracking discrepancies. "I've been watching her, and some things don't add up."

"Such as?" Melody asked.

"Today I saw her take money from the register during lunch rush and put it directly in her purse. When I asked about it, she said it was reimbursement for groceries, but I saw her buy those groceries with a restaurant credit card this morning."

"How much money could she have taken?" Lauren asked.

"Over time? Potentially thousands. And if Uncle Charlie Joe had found out..." Jackie let the implication hang in the air.

"You think Jovie killed Uncle Charlie Joe?" Melody asked.

"I think Jovie has been embezzling money to pay for her daughter's medical treatments. I think Uncle Charlie Joe might have discovered it. And I think desperate people sometimes do desperate things."

Lauren was quiet for a long time. "She did know his routines, had access to everything, would know how to make it look like natural causes."

"Plus, she's the one who 'found' him," Jackie added. "Perfect way to control the scene, make sure evidence was destroyed or contaminated."

"We should confront her," Melody said. "Present the evidence and observe her reactions. Guilty parties often reveal themselves through inconsistent explanations."

"Tomorrow," Jackie decided. "After the lunch rush. We'll ask to see the books and see how she responds."

Chapter Twelve

The last of the lunch customers had left. Lauren and Jackie exchanged a look. Neither of them was looking forward to this confrontation, but they knew it was the right thing. Plus, Jackie had faced worse in the courtroom many times.

The day before had been rough, but they had to put it behind them for now so they could be a united front.

"Jovie," Jackie said as the last customer left, "we need to see the financial records now. No more delays."

Jovie's face went pale. "I... I told you, they're not ready yet."

"They don't need to be perfect," Lauren said firmly. "We just need to understand the basic financial picture."

"Look, there might be some... discrepancies," Jovie said, her voice barely above a whisper. "But I can explain everything."

"What kind of discrepancies?" Jackie asked, her lawyer voice fully engaged.

"Money that's missing," Jovie admitted, tears forming in her eyes. "Money I took to pay for Emma's treatments. But I was going to pay it back, I swear. I've been working extra hours, bringing in my own customers... selling stuff online."

"How much money?" Lauren asked.

"Twelve thousand dollars," Jovie whispered. "Over the past eight months."

The silence that followed was deafening.

"Did Uncle Charlie Joe know?" Jackie asked.

"I... I think he suspected. He started asking questions about the books, wanting to see receipts, checking the register more carefully." Jovie was crying now. "But he never said anything directly. Maybe he understood about needing to take care of family."

"Or maybe he was planning to fire you," Jackie said coldly.

"Maybe he was planning to turn you in to the police," Lauren added.

"No!" Jovie said desperately. "Charlie Joe wasn't like that. He would have worked something out, given me time to pay it back."

"Unless he couldn't afford to be understanding," Jackie said. "Unless the restaurant was struggling and he needed every dollar."

"You think I killed him," Jovie said, the words hanging in the air like an accusation.

"We think you had motive, means, and opportunity," Jackie replied. "And we think the timing of his death was awfully convenient for someone who was embezzling money."

Jovie stared at them for a long moment, then started laughing. A bitter, hysterical sound.

"You think I killed Charlie Joe for twelve thousand dollars? When he was planning to leave me this entire restaurant?"

"What?" all three women asked simultaneously.

"Charlie Joe offered to sell me the restaurant six months ago. Said he was getting old, needed to think about retirement. Offered me a payment plan I could actually afford." Jovie wiped her eyes. "I turned him down because I couldn't take on that kind of debt with Emma's medical bills. Two weeks later, he told me he'd decided to leave it to family instead."

"He was going to sell it to you?" Lauren asked.

"For a fraction of what it's worth. Said I'd earned it, running the place all these years." Jovie's voice broke. "I chose my daughter's immediate medical needs over my long-term security. And Charlie Joe understood. He said family always comes first. That's when he started asking me if he should leave it to the two of you."

"Then why didn't you tell us this earlier or why didn't you come clean to him about what you had taken? You said he would have understood." Jackie demanded.

"Because I was ashamed! Because I stole money from a man who was trying to take care of me, trying to set me up for life!" Jovie sobbed. "Because I was afraid you'd think exactly what you're thinking now, that I'm some kind of criminal who would hurt the kindest man I've ever known."

Jackie felt her certainty crumbling. "If you didn't kill him, then who did?"

"I don't know," Jovie said. "But I know it wasn't natural causes, and I know it wasn't me. Charlie Joe was the only family I had left besides Emma. I would have done anything to protect him."

"Even steal from him?" Melody asked.

"Even steal from him," Jovie admitted. "But I would never, ever have hurt him. He was... he was like a brother to me."

Something had been nagging at Jackie since their first day, something that didn't quite add up. She hadn't pushed that first day for answers but now felt like time to ask the tough ones.

"Then can I ask you something about Uncle Charlie Joe's death?"

Jovie's expression immediately grew guarded as she wiped a tear. "What about it?"

"Harold mentioned it was sudden," Jackie said carefully. "A heart attack. But you were the one who found him, right?"

"I was." Jovie's voice was flat, matter-of-fact. "I came in at five like always do and found him slumped over his desk in the office."

"That must have been terrible," Lauren said softly. Any fight she had going into this was gone at the mention of her estranged uncle's death. Each day they worked here, and got to hear stories about him, added to Lauren's guilt at never getting to know him during his life.

"It was. But not just terrible, it was wrong," Jovie said looking directly at Jackie. "You're a lawyer. You know when things don't add up. Charlie Joe's death didn't add up."

Jackie felt her legal instincts sharpen. "What do you mean?"

Jovie glanced around the empty restaurant. "As I mentioned before, Charlie Joe was terrified those last few months. Phone calls at all hours, cars driving by slowly at night, people in town asking questions about his past. He started talking about his family more, asking if I thought his great-nieces could manage running the restaurant if something happened to him. You know, after he decided to leave it to y'all."

Melody looked up from her work, analytical mind engaged. "What kind of questions?"

"About how long he'd been here, whether he had family, what his life was like before he came to Prairie Rose. Professional-sounding folks, real polite, but persistent." Jovie's hand tightened around a coffee mug. "Charlie Joe started acting more paranoid, checking and rechecking the locks, testing that security camera system over and over."

"Tell us about the night he died," Jackie said, settling into her cross-examination mode.

"That's just it … something was off about that whole night. Charlie Joe usually locked up around eight o'clock, locked everything up tight. But that night, I drove by around ten because I'd forgotten my purse and needed Emma's insurance card out of it. I always hold her things when we go to the doctor. Anyway, the lights were on in the kitchen."

"Did you go in?" Lauren asked.

"I thought about it, but his truck was parked different than usual. Right up by the back door instead of his usual spot by the oak tree. And there was another car in the lot, one I didn't recognize, so it just didn't feel right. I left without my purse figuring I would just get in the morning."

Jackie felt her pulse quicken. "What kind of car?"

"Dark sedan, looked expensive. City car, not something you'd see around here much." Jovie's voice grew quieter. "I should have gone in. I've regretted it every day since. Maybe if I had, Charlie Joe would still be alive."

"What happened the next morning?" Melody asked, her notebook already out and taking systematic notes.

"As I said, I got here at five and the back door was unlocked. That was wrong. That was the first sign something was wrong. Charlie Joe never, ever left doors unlocked. Never. Plus, he would normally be tending the smoker at that time." Jovie stood up and walked toward the office door. She pushed it open. "Instead, I found him in there, slumped over his desk like he'd just fallen asleep, but..."

She paused, struggling with the memory.

"But what?" Jackie prompted gently.

"But his color was wrong. Not just pale but gray, almost blue. And there was a smell in the office, kind of chemical, medicinal. Dr. Thorne said it was probably medication Charlie Joe had taken for his chest pains, but that was nonsense."

"Why nonsense?" Lauren asked.

"Because Charlie Joe didn't take medication. Didn't trust doctors, didn't like pills. I'd been working with him for twenty years. If he'd been having chest pains, he would have told me. And if he'd been taking heart medication, I would have known."

"But he had gone to see Dr. Thorne a few weeks before," Lauren said.

"He told me it was just a simple checkup." Jovie looked confused.

"Dr. Thorne had said he told Charlie Joe to slow down, look at retiring."

"Why didn't he tell me?" Jovie mumbled.

Jackie walked over to the office door, examining the lock and frame with new eyes. "Who investigated his death?"

"Sheriff Henderson. But calling it an investigation is generous." Jovie's voice carried a bitter edge. "He was here maybe twenty minutes, asked me a few questions, said it looked like a straightforward heart attack, and that was it."

"No crime scene photos? No evidence collection?" Jackie's legal training was screaming that proper procedures hadn't been followed.

"Nothing. Dr. Thorne arrived, pronounced Charlie Joe dead, and said the symptoms I described were consistent with a massive heart attack." Jovie shook her head. "But I knew Charlie Joe. He was strong as a horse, worked fourteen-hour days without breaking a sweat."

Jackie felt the familiar thrill of a case coming together, the sense that lies were about to unravel and truth was about to emerge. "Jovie, I need to ask you directly. Do you think Uncle Charlie Joe was murdered?"

Jovie was quiet for a long moment, staring into the office. When she looked up, her eyes were hard with suppressed anger.

"I think Charlie Joe knew someone was coming for him. I think he tried to prepare for it as best he could. And I think whoever killed him made it look like natural causes because they knew nobody in Prairie Rose would ask too many questions about an old man dying alone."

"Why didn't you pursue this at the time?" Jackie asked.

"Because I'm a cook, not a detective. Because Sheriff Henderson made it clear he didn't want to hear my theories. And because I was scared." Jovie's voice grew smaller. "If someone killed Charlie Joe, and they thought I knew something..."

"But you're telling us now," Melody observed.

"Because you're family. And because Charlie Joe left you this place for a reason. Maybe he knew you'd be smart enough and stubborn enough to find out the truth." Jovie paled.

With all the talk of a possible murder, the embezzlement had been forgotten, for now. At least Jovie had been honest, or so Jackie hoped. They would find out the truth soon.

Lauren had been listening to this exchange with growing alarm. "If Uncle Charlie Joe was murdered, and we're investigating his death, doesn't that put us in danger too?"

"Probably. We've already gotten those threatening text messages and twice the smoker has been sabotaged," Jackie said grimly. "But it also gives us responsibility. Uncle Charlie Joe deserves justice."

"And," Melody added, consulting her notes, "if the same people who killed him are still active, they might see us as a threat regardless of whether we investigate. At least this way, we're gathering information instead of just waiting to be victims."

Jovie stood up and walked to the window, scanning the parking lot with practiced eyes. "There's something else you should know. Sheriff Henderson retired and left town not long after Charlie Joe died. Sold his house and moved to Florida real quick-like. It only took days for everything to go through, almost like it had been planned."

"That's suspicious timing," Jackie noted.

Jackie walked around the restaurant, seeing it with new eyes. This wasn't just a business they'd inherited, but it was a crime scene. Uncle Charlie Joe had died here, possibly murdered, and the investigation had been deliberately superficial. She'd had her suspicions from day one even if Harold had tried to lessen them.

"We need to document everything," Jackie said finally. "Every inconsistency in the official story, every suspicious detail, every person who might have been involved in covering this up."

"Are you sure we should be doing this?" Lauren asked. "Shouldn't we contact the current sheriff, let law enforcement handle it?"

"Sheriff Martinez seems honest," Jovie agreed. "But this involves his predecessor and the local doctor. He might not want to rock the boat, especially over something that happened before he took office."

"Plus," Melody added, "we have information that the official investigators either missed or ignored. We might be the only ones positioned to uncover the truth."

Jackie made a decision that would change everything. "We investigate this ourselves as we have been, but more actively. Quietly, carefully, but thoroughly. We owe Uncle Charlie Joe that much."

"What if we find proof that he was murdered?" Lauren asked.

"Then we take it to Sheriff Martinez and demand justice," Jackie replied. "But first, we need to understand what Uncle Charlie Joe was so afraid of, and why someone wanted him dead."

"And," Jovie added quietly, "we need to figure out if whoever killed him is still around, still watching, still dangerous."

As if summoned by her words, a dark sedan drove slowly past the restaurant windows. It was the same type of car Jovie had described seeing the night Uncle Charlie Joe died, but not the same as they'd seen Harrison Kale in. It completed one circuit of the parking lot, then disappeared down the highway.

"Did anyone else see that?" Lauren asked, her voice tight with anxiety.

"I saw it," Melody confirmed, already making a note of the time and license plate number she'd managed to glimpse.

"Third time this week," Jovie said grimly. "Different car each time, but same pattern. Slow drive-by, check out the parking lot, move on."

"Same as Harrison Kale," Lauren said.

"Someone's watching us," Jackie realized. "At least Kale made himself known. This person … didn't."

"Someone's been watching this place for weeks or longer," Jovie corrected. "The question is whether they're watching because they killed Charlie Joe, or because they're afraid someone might figure out that they killed Charlie Joe."

Jovie looked at the three ladies, "I know my confession doesn't change anything and you may not forgive me, but I hope that you can learn to trust me. We are on the same side with all of this."

Lauren and Jackie looked at each other. They weren't completely sold yet, but they had more pressing issues than Jovie.

"We can table that for now. First, we need to learn all we can about who this is watching us."

That's when they noticed a figure standing just outside. It was Tom Whitfield, and he was looking at them through the wide window that ran on that side of the building.

He didn't ride up on horseback this time. Instead, he appeared on foot, having apparently walked across the pasture and climbed through the fence line. Jackie only noticed him because Melody pointed toward him

"How long has he been there?" Jackie whispered.

"Unknown," Melody replied. "But his positioning suggests he was trying to overhear our discussion."

Jackie walked to the back door and opened it. "Tom. Can I help you with something?"

"Well, hey there, Jackie." Tom stepped closer to the building, his movements casual but his eyes alert. "Couldn't help but notice y'all seemed upset about something. Everything all right?"

"We're fine," Jackie said carefully.

"Good, good. It's just that I heard some concerning things in town. People saying you've been asking questions about Charlie Joe's death."

"People talk," Lauren said, joining Jackie at the door.

They'd only talked to a few people, one being Jovie. Despite their distrust of Jovie right now, Jackie doubted she would talk to Tom about them. He had to have overheard their conversations somehow.

"They do indeed. And sometimes they talk about things that might be better left alone." Tom's voice carried a warning. "Charlie Joe's death was investigated by proper authorities. Sheriff Henderson, Dr. Thorne. Good men who know this community. When they say natural causes, folks generally accept that and move on."

"Generally," Jackie repeated. "But not always?"

"Well, sometimes outsiders come in with their own ideas about how things should be handled. City folks who think they know better than local experts." Tom's gaze moved between Jackie and Lauren. "That kind of attitude can create... tension in a community."

"What kind of tension?" Melody asked, appearing in the doorway.

"The kind that makes people uncomfortable. The kind that makes neighbors wonder if new folks can be trusted to respect local customs and established ways of doing things." Tom looked directly at Melody, eyes narrowing. "Your great-uncle never quite learned that lesson. Always thought he could do things his own way, ignore community input, make decisions that affected other people without consulting anyone."

"Tom, you know darn good and well that's a lie. Charlie Joe loved this town and the community, and they loved him," Jovie said from behind Jackie.

"Jovie, now I'm not looking for trouble. Just looking out for y'all."

"So, what decisions had he made that affected others?" Jackie asked, getting back to Tom's statement.

"Such as buying land that disrupted established ranching operations. Such as running a business that attracted outsiders and changed the character of the area. Such as keeping secrets that made people wonder what he might be hiding." His tone held a hint of anger.

"What secrets?" Lauren asked.

Tom smiled, but it didn't reach his eyes. "The kind that make a man wake up in the middle of the night, checking locks, looking over his shoulder. Charlie Joe was scared of something those last few months. Anyone who paid attention could see it."

"How do you know that?" Jackie asked, looking back at Jovie who looked like she wanted to walk over and punch the arrogant cowboy.

"Because I pay attention to my neighbors," Tom replied. "Especially neighbors whose behavior affects my family's livelihood. Charlie Joe started acting paranoid, suspicious, talking about people watching him. Of course, when you've got secrets worth hiding, paranoia makes sense."

"You were watching him," Melody stated. It wasn't a question.

"I was being aware of activities that might affect my property and my family's security," Tom corrected. "Charlie Joe's increasingly erratic behavior was concerning to multiple community members."

"Concerning enough to do something about it?" Jackie asked.

Tom's expression hardened. "Concerning enough to hope that his family would be more reasonable about community relations and property management." He gestured toward their restaurant. "Hope that's proving to be the case."

"And if it's not?" Lauren asked.

"Then I suppose we'll discover whether outsiders can thrive in Prairie Rose when the local community isn't supportive," Tom said. "Small towns can be challenging places for people who don't fit in."

Jovie flinched slightly. Jackie placed a gentle hand on the woman which stopped her forward movement. Jackie had dealt with this type in the courtroom more times than she could count. It was best to let him think he had won.

As Tom walked away, Jackie realized they now had two major suspects: Jovie, who had financial motive and inside access, and Tom Whitfield, who had generational resentment and detailed knowledge of Uncle Charlie Joe's final months.

As evening approached and they prepared to close the restaurant, Jackie felt the weight of what they'd uncovered. Uncle Charlie Joe's death hadn't been natural and investigating it would put them all in danger.

Harold had hinted at it that first day in his office but they'd been too busy, too distracted to find out more about it. She was glad they had learned to trust Jovie enough to ask her about it. Though she would still keep her eye on the longtime employee who admitted to stealing. It seemed to be a worthy cause and all Jackie could do was hold her to paying it back.

But for the first time since her divorce, she felt like she was working on something that truly mattered.

Uncle Charlie Joe deserved justice. And the Rodriguez women were going to make sure he got it. Even if it put them in danger. They could handle themselves - look how far they'd already come together.

Chapter Thirteen

Jackie was elbow-deep in prep work for the lunch rush when her phone rang. She glanced at the caller ID and felt her stomach drop. Dawn Rodriguez, her mother. She hadn't spoken to Dawn since the lawyer's office meeting about Richard's latest financial maneuver three months ago.

"Don't answer it," Lauren said without looking up from the vegetables she was chopping. "We're too busy."

"I have to answer it," Jackie replied, already dreading the conversation. "If I don't, she'll just keep calling until I do."

She wiped her hands on her apron and stepped outside to take the call. "Hi, Mom."

"Jackie, darling, finally! I've been trying to reach you for days." Dawn's voice carried that particular tone that meant she was building up to something dramatic. "I've been beside myself with worry."

"I've been busy, Mom. Lauren and I are running Uncle Charlie Joe's restaurant."

"Yes, I heard about that ridiculous inheritance situation. Honestly, what was that man thinking, forcing you to work with Lauren?" Dawn's voice sharpened with disapproval. "You know she's always resented your success."

Jackie felt familiar tension building in her shoulders. "Mom, it's more complicated than that."

"Is it? Because from where I'm sitting, it looks like Lauren manipulated a vulnerable old man into leaving you both something that would force you to support her financially."

"That's not what happened."

"Isn't it? She's been struggling for years, Jackie. A single mother with a special needs child, living paycheck to paycheck. And suddenly Uncle Charlie Joe, who barely spoke to our family, leaves you both a restaurant that you have to run together? It's awfully convenient."

Jackie watched through the window as Lauren efficiently organized the lunch prep, her movements precise. Melody sat at a corner table, updating their inventory spreadsheets with the kind of focused attention that had helped them streamline their operations significantly.

"Lauren didn't manipulate anyone. Just like you said, he barely spoke to our family. Though I thought you talked to him from time to time."

"I did but he grew distant the last several years."

"And I know for a fact that Lauren hadn't spoken to him in years either," Jackie said firmly. "And Melody isn't a burden. She's actually been incredibly helpful and … wonderful. Sweet, smart. I'm enjoying getting to know her."

"Oh, honey." Dawn's voice took on that patronizing tone that made Jackie feel like a naïve child. "I know you want to see the best in people, but you can't let family guilt cloud your judgment. You've worked too hard to rebuild your life after Richard's betrayal to throw it away on some fantasy about barbecue and sisterly bonding."

"I'm not throwing anything away."

"You're throwing away your career, your social standing, your future security. For what? To play house with a sister who's never liked you and a niece who..." Dawn paused, clearly choosing her words carefully.

"Who what?" Jackie's voice had gone dangerously quiet.

"Who has limitations, darling. I'm not being cruel, just realistic. Melody is sweet, but she requires constant accommodation and care. Is that really how you want to spend your fifties?"

Jackie felt anger flare in her chest, not just at the words, but at the familiar way Dawn could make her doubt herself and the people she cared about. However, now she was seeing her through different eyes. "Melody doesn't require constant care. She's twenty-two years old, she's brilliant, and she's probably more capable than either of us."

"Jackie, please. You're being defensive because you know I'm right. Lauren has always used Melody's condition to avoid taking responsibility for her own choices."

"Stop." The word came out sharper than Jackie intended. "Just stop, Mom."

"I'm only trying to protect you. Someone has to think practically about your situation."

"My situation is fine. Better than fine, actually."

"Living above a restaurant in some tiny town in the middle of nowhere? Working as a short-order cook? That's fine?" Dawn's voice rose with incredulity. "You were a successful attorney, Jackie. You had a beautiful home, social status, and a reputation as one powerful attorney."

"I had a marriage that was a lie, a career that made me miserable, and a reputation based on representing people I didn't respect," Jackie interrupted. "And I was so focused on maintaining all of that that I forgot how to actually connect with the people I love."

"People you love? Lauren made her choice thirty-five years ago when she chose your father's side over family loyalty. And now you're rewarding her for it."

"I didn't choose your side because I thought you were right, Mom. I chose your side because I was eighteen and scared and I thought loyalty meant picking a team." Jackie paced across the small porch, her voice growing stronger. "But loyalty should mean supporting each other even when we disagree, not demanding that people choose sides in conflicts that aren't theirs."

"That's very idealistic, but —"

"It's not idealistic. It's what Lauren and I are learning to do now. We disagree about plenty of things, but we're not asking each other to choose between competing loyalties anymore."

Through the window, she could see Lauren glancing in her direction with obvious concern. Their lunch prep was perfectly coordinated now. They'd developed an intuitive understanding of each other's working rhythms that made their early conflicts seem almost ridiculous.

Things still weren't perfect or resolved between them, but they were learning.

"Jackie, I'm worried about you," Dawn said, her tone shifting to wounded concern. "This isn't like you. You've always been the practical one, the one who thinks things through."

"I have thought it through. I'm happier here than I've been in years."

"You're happy playing restaurant with your sister and her damaged daughter?"

The words hit Jackie like a physical blow. "Melody is not damaged. And even if she were, that wouldn't make her less valuable or less deserving of love and respect."

"I didn't mean —"

"Yes. Yes, you did. You meant exactly that." Jackie took a deep breath, feeling something shift inside her chest. "Mom, I love you, but I can't do this anymore."

"Do what?"

"I can't keep letting you make me feel guilty for caring about people you don't approve of. I can't keep listening to you tear down Lauren and Melody because it makes you feel better about the choices you made during the divorce."

"I never —"

"You did. You do. Every time we talk, you find some way to remind me that Lauren 'chose Dad' and that I was right to 'choose you.' But the truth is, we were kids dealing with an adult problem, and neither of us should have had to choose anything."

Dawn was silent for a long moment. When she spoke again, her voice was smaller, more uncertain. "I was hurt, Jackie. Your father and I... it was very painful."

"I know it was. But Lauren and I paid the price for that pain, and we're still paying it. And I won't let Melody pay it too. Heck, even Alec and Caden are paying for it."

"I don't understand what's happened to you."

"I'm learning to be part of a family instead of managing one from a distance. I'm learning that caring about people doesn't make you weak or naïve. It makes you human."

The back door of the restaurant opened, and Lauren stepped out. "Everything okay?" she asked quietly.

Jackie looked at her sister, really looked at her. Lauren's face showed genuine concern, not curiosity or judgment. She wasn't trying to eavesdrop or control the conversation; she was simply offering support.

"Mom, I have to go," Jackie said. "We're about to open for lunch."

"Jackie, wait. I think we should talk about this more. Maybe I could drive down and see this restaurant, meet Melody properly."

"Maybe," Jackie said carefully. "But only if you can come with an open mind and a closed mouth about what you think I should be doing with my life."

"That's rather harsh."

"It's honest. I love you, Mom, but I won't let you poison this the way you've poisoned my relationships with Alec and Caden."

"I never —"

"You did. Every time they visited, you found ways to criticize their choices, their girlfriends, their career paths. You made them feel like they had to defend their lives to you instead of just sharing them with you."

Dawn was quiet again. Finally, she sighed. "I suppose I have been rather... opinionated."

"You've been controlling. And critical. And it's driven people away." Jackie's voice softened slightly. "I don't want to be driven away, Mom. But I also won't sacrifice my relationship with Lauren and Melody to manage your feelings about the divorce."

"I see."

"Do you? Because this is important. Lauren is my sister, Melody is my niece, and they're both important to me. If you can accept that and treat them with respect, then you're welcome in my life. If you can't, then we're going to have a problem."

Lauren had moved closer during the conversation, close enough to offer silent support but far enough away to give Jackie privacy. It was a perfect demonstration of the kind of emotional intelligence that Jackie was still learning. To be present without being intrusive.

"I suppose I could try to be more... diplomatic," Dawn said finally.

"I don't need you to be diplomatic, Mom. I need you to be kind. There's a difference."

"Yes, I suppose there is."

"Look, I really do have to go. We've got customers waiting. But think about what I said, okay? And if you decide you want to visit, call first. Don't just show up expecting everyone to accommodate your schedule."

"All right, Jackie. I... I love you, you know."

"I love you too, Mom. But love isn't enough if it comes with conditions and requirements."

After she hung up, Jackie stood on the porch for a moment, feeling emotionally drained but also strangely liberated. She'd never spoken to her mother that directly before, never set such clear boundaries.

"Rough conversation?" Lauren asked gently.

"Very rough. But necessary." Jackie looked at her sister. "She said some things about you and Melody that were... unacceptable."

"What kinds of things?"

"The kinds of things that made me realize I've been letting her shape my opinions about people for way too long." Jackie managed a small smile. "Including you."

"Ah." Lauren nodded knowingly. "Mom never really forgave me for siding with Dad during the divorce."

"And I never really forgave you for not siding with Mom. But the truth is, we were both just trying to survive a bad situation with limited options."

"And now?"

"Now we're adults who can choose our own relationships instead of inheriting them from our parents' conflicts." Jackie straightened her shoulders. "Speaking of which, are you ready for the lunch rush? Because I have a feeling today's going to test all our new systems."

"Ready," Lauren said, then hesitated. "Jackie? Thank you. For standing up for Melody and me."

"Thank you for not making me choose between you and Mom. That's not a choice anyone should have to make."

"No, it's not."

Before they stepped into the restaurant, movement at the fence line caught their attention. There stood their neighbor Tom, a smirk spread across his face. How much had he heard?

Lauren and Jackie exchanged a look then looked at their creepy neighbor. Tom tipped his hat then rode off on his horse.

"Why is he always listening to us? He just always seems to be around," Lauren said.

"He is a strange guy, but I'm just thankful he didn't come threaten us again," Jackie said. "Ready?"

"Ready."

As they headed back inside, Jackie felt lighter somehow. The conversation with Mom had been difficult, but it had also clarified something important: she was done letting other people's fears and resentments determine her relationships.

And for the first time in thirty-five years, Jackie was choosing her sister.

"Hey Lauren?" she called as they resumed their prep work.

"Yeah?"

"Next time Mom calls, would you like to talk to her? She needs to understand that you're not going anywhere, and neither am I."

Lauren's smile was worth every difficult word Jackie had said to their mother.

"I'd like that," Lauren said. "I'd like that very much."

As the first lunch customers began arriving, Jackie realized that some of the most important work they did at the restaurant happened not at the stove or the register, but in the conversations that cleared the air and opened hearts.

Chapter Fourteen

Their second Sunday morning at Charlie Joe's BBQ Shack began like any other day with Jackie rolling out of bed at 4:30 AM, the familiar ritual of coffee and prep work, the comforting rhythm of starting the fires. But by noon, it was clear that this Sunday would be different from anything they'd experienced so far.

"Sweet Mother of Pearl," Jovie breathed, staring out the front window at the parking lot that was rapidly filling beyond capacity. "I haven't seen it like this since before Charlie Joe passed."

Cars were parked along the highway shoulder, families were spreading blankets under the oak tree, and a steady stream of people kept arriving despite the fact that they'd already served more customers than they usually saw in an entire day.

"How many people go to church in this town?" Jackie asked, frantically assembling pulled pork sandwiches while Lauren managed the register and Melody tried to keep track of orders.

"Most of them," said Maria Santos, who had arrived two hours early to help and was now working the drink station like a woman possessed.

"Table six is still waiting for their brisket," Lauren called out, sweat beading on her forehead despite the October coolness.

"Brisket's gone," Jovie replied from the kitchen. "I started the backup this morning, but it won't be ready for another five hours, maybe six."

"What do we tell people?" Jackie asked, feeling panic rising in her chest.

"We tell them the truth," said a familiar voice. Frank Kowalski appeared at the pickup window, wearing what was obviously his Sunday best with a pressed shirt and a bolo tie. "Charlie Joe used to run out of brisket every Sunday. Folks expected it. Made the pulled pork feel special."

Behind him, Jackie could see a line of people that stretched to the door and beyond. Families with children, elderly couples holding hands, groups of teenagers who looked like they'd come straight from youth group. The noise level was unlike anything they'd experienced. Not chaotic, but warm and conversational, the sound of a community gathering.

"Mrs. Prescott?" A young woman with three small children approached the counter. "I'm Sarah Carlton, my kids go to school with the Blake children? You know Annie and her mother, Claire Rigby. Ms. Claire said you might have some of that coleslaw my great-grandmother used to make here."

Jackie looked at Lauren helplessly. They'd made coleslaw using Uncle Charlie Joe's recipe, but she had no idea whose grandmother might have made it originally.

"Charlie Joe learned that recipe from Mrs. Blankenship," Maria called out. "Sarah's great-grandmother. She taught half the ladies in town how to make it, but Charlie Joe was the only one who got the proportions exactly right."

Sarah's face lit up. "Really? I didn't want to get my hopes up. Could I get extra coleslaw then? For my mom? She's been craving it since Grandma passed then we recently heard that Charlie Joe had learned it years ago from Grandma."

As Jackie ladled an extra portion of coleslaw, she felt something shift inside her chest. This wasn't just about serving food. It was about preserving memories, maintaining connections, being part of something larger than herself.

"Jackie!" Lauren's voice cut through her thoughts. "We need more sweet tea. Like, a lot more."

"I'm on it!"

The next hour passed in a blur of controlled chaos. They ran out of potato salad, then green beans, then rolls. Jovie started a batch of emergency cornbread while Maria organized a system for managing the line. Lauren started working on more sides while Jackie ran out to the smoker to pull more ribs, chicken and sausage.

Several customers offered to help bus tables, and someone's teenage son started directing parking in the lot.

"This is insane," Jackie muttered as she carried a tray of drinks to a family seated under the oak tree.

"This is community," corrected the father, a man about Jackie's age wearing a pastor's collar. "I'm Reverend Williams from Prairie Rose Methodist. Charlie Joe used to cater our church picnics."

"Oh nice."

"Every year for the last twenty years." Reverend Williams smiled. "The congregation's been praying for whoever inherited this place. We were hoping they'd understand what Charlie Joe built here."

"What did he build?" Jackie asked, genuinely curious, though she had an idea. She'd been hearing it with every customer that they served.

"A place where everyone belongs. Where the banker sits next to the janitor, where kids can run around while parents catch up with neighbors, where nobody goes hungry if they can't afford to pay." The reverend gestured around the crowded restaurant grounds. "Charlie Joe understood that food is just the excuse. The real business here is bringing people together."

Back inside, Melody had stationed herself at a corner table with her laptop and was frantically taking notes. "Order patterns," she explained when Lauren asked what she was doing. "Customer preferences, timing intervals, logistical bottlenecks. If we're going to handle crowds like this regularly, we need data."

"Regularly?" Jackie looked around at the organized chaos. "This can't be normal."

"Actually," said a woman Jackie didn't recognize, "this is pretty typical for a Sunday after church lets out. Charlie Joe always had a crowd like this. We just haven't had anywhere to go since he passed. Jovie couldn't manage this crowd alone and we didn't come last week to give y'all a break. But we missed this."

The woman introduced herself as Betty Walsh, former president of the Prairie Rose Chamber of Commerce. "The whole town's been talking about you girls. Some folks were worried you'd change things, make it all modern and fancy. But Maria Santos has been telling everyone you're doing things the right way."

"The right way?" Lauren asked.

"Charlie Joe's way, of course. Good food, fair prices, treating people like family." Betty looked around approvingly. "Though you might want to think about expanding your seating. And maybe hiring more help."

"We're still figuring things out," Jackie said diplomatically.

"Well, figure fast," Betty advised with a smile. "Because word's getting out beyond Prairie Rose. My sister from Fredericksburg is driving over next weekend with her book club."

As the afternoon wore on, Jackie began to notice patterns in the crowd. Three generations of the Martinez family occupied two large tables. The Rigby-Blake family had brought friends, who had brought their friends, creating an ever-expanding network of connections.

A group of teenagers had claimed the picnic tables under the oak tree and were playing cards while waiting for their food. Several older men gathered around Frank Kowalski's usual table, discussing what sounded like local politics with the passionate intensity that small town issues always generated.

Several customers exchanged uncomfortable glances as they watched Sheriff Martinez helping his elderly father navigate the buffet-style serving system they'd improvised, but Jackie noticed how his eyes kept finding Lauren throughout the afternoon, and how Lauren seemed to glow whenever he was nearby.

Jackie smiled to herself as she watched their sweet but distant interaction throughout the afternoon.

"It's like a weekly reunion," Lauren observed during a brief lull.

"It is a weekly reunion," confirmed Mrs. Thorne from the general store. Dr. Thorne was her son. "Has been for twenty years. Charlie Joe never advertised it, never made a big deal about it, but every Sunday this place turned into the town's living room."

"What happened when Uncle Charlie Joe passed?" Melody asked.

"We tried going to other places, but it wasn't the same," Mrs. Thorne said sadly. "The food was fine, but there was no... heart to it. No sense that we all belonged there together."

As closing time approached, Sheriff Martinez appeared at the counter during a brief lull. Over the past week, he'd become a regular customer. Usually, he ordered a sandwich and a sweet tea to-go. Jackie had also noticed that his visits seemed to coincide with times when Lauren was working the front of house.

"Busy day," he observed, but his attention was focused entirely on Lauren.

"Our biggest yet," Lauren replied, tucking a strand of hair behind her ear with a slight blush. "I never imagined we'd be serving this many people."

"You're building something special here," he said quietly. "Charlie Joe would be proud."

"Thank you," Lauren said, her voice softer than usual. "That means a lot."

Jackie watched the exchange with growing interest. The chemistry between her sister and the sheriff was undeniable, even if Lauren seemed determined to ignore it.

"Well, y'all take care. I'm going to get my father home now. Thanks for a wonderful experience." He tipped his hat but never took his eyes off of Lauren.

"Night, Sheriff." Lauren blushed.

It was nearly seven PM when they finally served their last customer, a young couple with a crying baby who looked exhausted and grateful for hot food and kind words. As they cleaned up, Jackie tried to process what they'd just experienced.

"How many people did we serve today?" she asked Melody.

"One hundred and forty-seven," Melody replied, consulting her notes. "Nearly triple our previous daily record."

"And we ran out of almost everything," Lauren added.

"But nobody complained," Maria pointed out. "People were happy to wait, happy to help, happy to be here."

"Why?" Jackie asked. "I mean, the food is good, but it's not magical. What makes people willing to wait two hours for a sandwich?"

"Because it's not about the sandwich," said a voice from the doorway. They turned to see Birdie Hutchins entering with a covered dish. They had only met her briefly today in the chaos. "It's about the place, the people, the feeling that you matter to somebody."

"Mrs. Hutchins," Lauren said warmly. "You left early. I had hoped to talk to you more."

"Yes, I don't like crowds much. Brought you some dessert, though. Ezra's famous peach cobbler recipe." Birdie set the dish on the counter. "Figured you might be too tired to make anything sweet after a day like today."

"That's incredibly thoughtful," Jackie said, genuinely touched.

"Charlie Joe used to serve this every Sunday," Birdie explained. "Said people needed something sweet to end their week right and start their new week hopeful."

"Did you make it for him?" Melody asked.

"Sometimes, but he had the recipe memorized."

"We need to make this then each week," Laure said.

As they sat around one of the tables sharing Birdie's cobbler, Jackie felt a contentment she hadn't experienced in years. Her feet hurt, her back ached, and she smelled like barbecue smoke, but she also felt... useful. Connected. Part of something meaningful.

"I called my sons today," she said suddenly, then felt surprised that she'd spoken the thought aloud. It was before the crowds started and she had just a moment to herself.

"Oh?" Lauren looked up from her cobbler. "How are Alec and Caden?"

"Busy. Successful. Still politely distant." Jackie pushed cobbler around her plate. "But for the first time in years, I had something interesting to tell them. Not just work drama or divorce updates, but... this. What we're building here."

"What did they say?" Melody asked.

"Alec said it sounded 'surprisingly fulfilling for a career change.' Caden asked if we needed a website." Jackie smiled ruefully. "Classic responses. But they also both said they might visit for Thanksgiving if we're still doing this."

"Of course we'll still be doing this," Lauren said firmly. "After today, how could we not?"

"Today was special," Jackie said. "But it was also overwhelming. If every Sunday is like this..."

"Every Sunday should be like this," Jovie interrupted. "I know I keep saying it, everyone keeps saying it but this is what Charlie Joe built. This is what Prairie Rose has been missing since he passed."

Birdie nodded. "Charlie Joe always said that Sunday dinner was sacred, not just for religious reasons, but because it was when families and communities came together. When people remembered they belonged to each other."

"The logistics are going to be challenging," Melody said practically. "We need more seating, additional staff, better inventory management."

"We need to expand," Jackie said, the business side of her brain engaging. "Add more outdoor seating, maybe a covered pavilion for large groups."

"We need to be careful not to lose what makes this special," Lauren cautioned. "Growth can destroy authenticity if you're not careful."

"Smart girl," Birdie said approvingly. "Charlie Joe turned down opportunities to franchise, to open additional locations, to partner with larger operations. He always said the moment you try to replicate magic, you kill it."

"So, we grow thoughtfully," Jackie said. "We expand capacity without losing character."

"We hire people who understand the mission," Lauren added. "Like Maria."

"We optimize systems without compromising values," Melody concluded.

They thanked Birdie for the cobbler and she promised to stop by again soon.

As they finished cleaning up and prepared to head upstairs, Jackie realized that today had changed something fundamental about how she viewed the restaurant. It wasn't just a business they'd inherited, it was a responsibility they'd accepted. A trust that Uncle Charlie Joe had placed in them to continue something he'd spent decades building.

"Next Sunday," she said to Lauren as they climbed the stairs, "we'll be ready."

"Ready for what?" Lauren asked.

"Ready to prove that Uncle Charlie Joe was right about us. That we can do this. That we can take care of this community the way he did."

"Even if it means working seven days a week and running ourselves ragged?"

"Especially then," Jackie said. "Because for the first time in years, I feel like I'm doing something that actually matters."

"Me too," Lauren said smiling.

Above them, Melody was already making lists of supply orders, staffing needs, expansion possibilities. The Sunday crowd had shown them what Charlie Joe's BBQ Shack could be at its full potential. Now they had to figure out how to make that potential sustainable.

But as Jackie settled into bed, listening to the sounds of the Hill Country night, she felt optimistic about their chances. Today had proven that Prairie Rose was ready to welcome them fully into Uncle Charlie Joe's legacy, despite what Tom kept saying to them.

The question now was whether they were ready to fully embrace that legacy, with all the responsibility and joy it entailed.

Chapter Fifteen

It was Lauren who noticed the cattle first. She was taking out the morning trash when she saw them. A dozen head of cattle grazing peacefully in what should have been their parking lot.

"Um, Jackie?" she called. "We have a problem."

Jackie stepped outside to find their customer parking area occupied by cattle, all wearing Whitfield Ranch brands. The animals seemed perfectly content, but their presence effectively blocked access to the restaurant.

"He can't be serious," Jackie muttered.

That's when Tom Whitfield appeared, riding his horse from the direction of his ranch with the casual air of someone who hadn't just sabotaged their business. A cattle dog followed closely with a look that said he was ready to get to work.

"Morning, ladies," he called out cheerfully. "Looks like some of my cattle wandered onto your property. Darn things must have found a break in the fence line."

"Those cattle didn't wander anywhere," Jackie said angrily. "You drove them here deliberately."

"Now, that's a serious accusation," Tom said, dismounting and walking among the cattle with practiced ease. "Course, proving deliberate action versus cattle doing what cattle naturally do... that might be challenging."

"What do you want, Tom?" Lauren asked.

"Same thing I've always wanted. A reasonable conversation about land use that makes sense for the community." Tom began gently herding the cattle, but slowly, making no real effort to clear the parking lot quickly. The dog paced impatiently waiting for his command. "See, cattle have been grazing this area for over a hundred years. Sometimes they get confused when their traditional grazing lands get turned into commercial operations."

"This is harassment," Jackie said.

"This is ranching," Tom corrected. "Cattle go where they've always gone, especially when fencing isn't properly maintained. Of course, if the property were returned to appropriate agricultural use, this kind of confusion wouldn't happen."

"How long is this going to take?" Melody asked, watching the cattle with scientific interest.

"Oh, hard to say. Cattle move at their own pace, especially when they're comfortable in familiar territory." Tom's smile was infuriating. "Could be hours. Could be all day. Depends on lots of factors."

"If you used the dog, I imagine it wouldn't take you long at all," Jackie said crossing her arms as she watched Tom slowly circle the cattle.

"We have customers coming for lunch soon," Lauren said.

"Well, that is a problem. Again, if this property were being used for its intended purpose, sustainable cattle operations, customer access wouldn't be an issue." Tom continued his leisurely herding. "Amazing how many problems get solved when land is used the way it was meant to be used."

It took Tom two hours to clear the cattle from their parking lot, and he managed to do it just as their lunch customers were giving up and driving away. The timing was too perfect to be accidental.

"This is escalating," Jackie said as they watched the last customer leave in frustration.

"He's testing us," Melody observed. "Determining our response to increasing levels of harassment."

"He always seems to do this when Jovie isn't here too," Jackie noted.

"He does. What's the next level?" Lauren asked.

They found out the following day when their deliveries started going missing.

"Honest mistake," Tom explained when Jackie called to demand their brisket back. "Delivery driver got confused about addresses. These rural routes can be tricky for city folks."

"The driver's been making this delivery for three years," Jackie replied.

"Well, sometimes people get new instructions they didn't expect," Tom said. "I'll have my boys bring your meat over later today. Might take a while though. We're pretty busy with ranch work."

The meat arrived at 4 PM. It had been stored in Tom's freezer, but Jackie noticed it smelled slightly off, as if the temperature control hadn't been perfect.

"We can't serve this," Jovie said after examining the brisket. "It's not spoiled exactly, but it's not up to our standards."

"So, we lose a day's revenue and have to make an emergency grocery run," Jackie said grimly.

Wednesday brought "accidentally" severed phone lines that left them unable to take reservations or process credit card payments. Thursday saw their propane delivery truck develop mysterious engine trouble right at the entrance to their property, blocking access for two hours.

"It's systematic," Melody observed as they dealt with the latest crisis. "He's targeting our supply chain, our communications, our customer access. Classic economic warfare designed to make our business unsustainable."

"And it's all just barely legal," Jackie added. "Accidents, mistakes, equipment failures. Nothing we can prove is deliberate sabotage."

"Plus, he's doing it in ways that make us look unreliable to customers," Lauren said. "People don't want to eat at a restaurant that can't keep phone service or guarantee they'll have food available."

"And after the great Sunday we had," Jackie noted.

Friday's "accident" was more serious. At 5 AM Jackie found that their water supply had been "accidentally" contaminated when Tom's cattle had somehow broken through multiple fence barriers and spent the night in the creek upstream from their property. The creek fed their well.

"Cattle waste in the water supply," the health inspector explained. "I'll have to red-tag your facility until you can prove the water is safe for food service."

"How long will that take?" Lauren asked.

"Testing takes 48 hours minimum. More if we find any bacterial contamination."

"So, we're closed for the rest of the week," Jackie said.

"Unless you can find an alternative water source," the inspector said sympathetically. "This kind of thing happens sometimes with rural restaurants."

That afternoon, Tom Whitfield appeared at their door with an expression of false concern.

"Heard about your water troubles," he said. "Terrible shame. Course, this kind of contamination issue is exactly why commercial food operations don't mix well with traditional ranching areas."

"Your cattle contaminated our water," Jackie said bluntly.

"Cattle go where cattle go," Tom replied. "Amazing how they always seem to find their way to water sources, especially during dry spells. Of course, if this property were returned to appropriate agricultural use, livestock access to water wouldn't be a contamination issue."

"Why the sudden escalation, Tom?" Jackie asked.

"Oh, you think I'm doing this on purpose." He threw his head back with a guttural laugh. "This is just a normal week in ranching, which you'd know if you were a rancher."

"How much?" Lauren asked suddenly.

"Excuse me?"

"How much are you offering for the property? Let's hear your actual number."

Tom's eyes lit up. "Well, given the challenges you've been having with infrastructure, supply chain issues, regulatory compliance... I'd say fair market value would be around four hundred thousand."

"The property is worth over a million," Jackie said.

"That's the tax assessment value, which assumes successful commercial operation," Tom corrected. "But given the operational difficulties you've been experiencing, the realistic value for quick sale to a buyer who can handle the challenges would be significantly lower."

"You mean the challenges you've been creating," Melody said.

"I mean the challenges that naturally arise when incompatible land uses conflict with each other," Tom replied smoothly. "Those challenges disappear when the land is returned to appropriate agricultural use."

"We're not selling," Jackie said firmly.

"Yet," Tom said. "But business pressures have a way of changing people's perspectives. Amazing how quickly folks can go from confident to desperate when their revenue stream gets disrupted."

As Tom left, Jackie realized they were facing a deliberate campaign to force them out of business. Tom Whitfield wasn't just a greedy neighbor. He was a methodical adversary who understood exactly how to make their lives impossible.

"He's not going to stop," she said to Lauren and Melody.

"No," Lauren agreed. "And it's going to get worse before it gets better."

"Unless we find a way to stop him first," Melody added.

Chapter Sixteen

"We need more sweet tea mix and at least fifty pounds of ice," Jovie announced after the lunch rush on Thursday. "Plus, we're running low on napkins and takeout containers."

They had finally been able to reopen on Tuesday and so far Tom hadn't pulled any of his tricks. With the reopening, they had a crowd. Everyone commented on how they had missed the brisket sandwich.

"Shopping trip," Jackie said, pulling off her apron. "Lauren, want to come explore downtown Prairie Rose?"

"I'll stay here with Melody," Lauren said. "She's redesigning the storage system again, and I want to make sure she doesn't reorganize us into efficiency paralysis."

"I heard that," Melody called from behind a stack of supply boxes. "And paralysis is impossible when the current system has fifteen separate inefficiencies."

Jackie chuckled as she grabbed her keys and left. She drove into downtown Prairie Rose with a growing sense of curiosity about the place Uncle Charlie Joe had called home for thirty years.

She had only driven through it previously but never had a chance to see much.

The town center was a mix of old and new with historic buildings housing modern businesses, antique shops next to trendy cafes, and a courthouse that looked like it belonged in a Norman Rockwell painting.

Her first stop was Thorne's General Store, a family-owned establishment that appeared to have been selling everything from hardware to groceries since the 1940s. The elderly man behind the counter looked up when she entered, his face lighting with recognition. She'd already met his wife and son, but not Mr. Thorne himself.

"You must be one of Charlie Joe's girls," he said warmly. "I'm Bill Thorne. Heard you took over the restaurant."

"Jackie Prescott," she said, extending her hand. "We're still learning the ropes."

"Charlie Joe would be proud. That man loved that place more than life itself." Bill extended his hand to hers. "So, what can I do you for today?"

"A few supplies." She handed him the list.

He nodded and began gathering the supplies from her list.

"He loved this whole town. Always first to help when someone was in trouble," he said absently.

"What kind of trouble?" Jackie asked.

"Oh, you know things like … oh, when Mrs. Silver's roof leaked for months, so of course Charlie Joe organized a work party to fix it including feeding everyone who helped. Then the Hale family lost their house in a fire, and Charlie Joe ran a fundraiser, fed folks for free while they collected donations." Bill shook his head admiringly. "Never wanted credit, never asked for anything back. He just wanted to feed and take care of people."

"He sounds like a good man."

"The best." Bill's expression grew more serious. "Which is why some of us have been worried about all the strangers asking questions lately."

Jackie's attention sharpened. To date her knowledge was limited to their experiences and what Jovie had told them. Getting an additional point of view could help with these puzzle pieces.

"What kind of strangers?"

"Well-dressed folks, driving fancy cars, saying they're doing research about local businesses." Bill rang up her purchases. "But they're asking mighty specific questions about Charlie Joe's personal life. How long he'd been here, whether he had family, what he did before he came to Prairie Rose."

"What did you tell them?"

"Same thing everyone else told them. Charlie Joe was a private man who minded his own business and helped his neighbors. That's all any of us knew, and all we needed to know." Bill leaned across the counter. "But between you and me, some of these folks didn't seem satisfied with that answer."

"How many different people have been asking?"

"At least three that I've seen personally. Probably more I haven't." Bill handed her the receipt. "You girls be careful. Charlie Joe was running from something when he came here, and whatever it was might not be finished with him yet."

Jackie's next stop was the Prairie Rose Community Bank, ostensibly to ask about business accounts but really to see if anyone else had been inquiring about Uncle Charlie Joe's financial affairs. The teller, a young woman named Sadie, was happy to help but couldn't discuss specific account information.

"I can tell you that several people have asked about Mr. Wagner's accounts," Sadie said quietly. "We can't give out any information, of course, but it's unusual to have so much interest in one customer."

"What kind of people?" Jackie asked.

"Lawyers, they said. Claimed they were settling his estate." Sadie glanced around to make sure no one was listening. "But Mr. Castellanos said their paperwork didn't look right. Too generic, missing details that real estate lawyers would have. Plus, I know that Harold Wilson is overseeing Charlie Joe's affairs. Harold is my uncle."

Jackie thanked Sadie and walked back to her car, increasingly troubled by the pattern that was emerging. Uncle Charlie Joe's secrets weren't just attracting threats. They were drawing systematic investigation from multiple sources.

Her final stop was supposed to be the hardware store for a replacement part for the ice machine, but as she walked down Main Street, she noticed someone watching her from across the street. A man in a dark suit who seemed to be pretending to read a newspaper while actually tracking her movement.

Jackie ducked into the Annie Café, a cozy establishment with mismatched furniture and the kind of atmosphere that invited lingering. The owner, a woman in her fifties with paint-stained fingers and bright earrings, looked up from the espresso machine.

"You're Jackie Prescott, right?" She asked with a smile. "I'm Annie Rigby-Blake. I'm Claire Rigby's daughter. Mom can't stop talking about the pulled pork she had the other day."

"Your mother is very kind," Jackie said, settling at a table with a view of the street. "You came in on Sunday too, right?"

"Yes, that's right. The whole clan. We are so happy to have Charlie Joe's as our Sunday place. Can I get you a coffee or latte?"

"Yes, please. Coffee. I'm hiding out for a minute. There's someone following me."

Annie's expression immediately shifted to concern as she grabbed a mug, filling it then bringing it to the table for Jackie. "Dark suit, fake newspaper?"

"You've seen him before?"

"Yeah, the last few days. Today he's been standing there nursing a single coffee for the past hour. Gave me the creeps, asking casual questions about Charlie Joe's restaurant." Annie sat down across from her. "He wanted to know about your family, how long you'd been in town, whether you seemed like the type to sell quickly."

"What did you tell him?"

"That I'd never met you, but anyone Charlie Joe chose as family was probably worth knowing." Annie glanced toward the window. "He's still out there, by the way. Look at him. Pretending to window shop at the antique store."

"This is getting ridiculous," Jackie muttered. "How many people are watching us?"

"More than there should be," Annie said grimly. "My husband works for the county assessor's office. He says there have been at least six different inquiries about your property in the past three weeks. People checking tax records, ownership history, zoning restrictions."

"For development purposes?"

"That's what they claimed. But Jim said some of the questions were weird, like asking about previous owners, when the land was first purchased, whether there were any liens or encumbrances dating back decades."

Jackie felt more pieces of the puzzle clicking into place. "They're not just interested in buying the property. They're researching Uncle Charlie Joe's history."

"Seems like it. And Jim said one of the inquiries came from a private investigation firm in Dallas."

Through the window, Jackie watched the man in the suit finally give up his surveillance and walk away. But instead of feeling relieved, she felt more exposed. If there were private investigators involved, the situation was more serious than threatening texts and property developers.

She turned to the friendly woman, unsure of who she could trust, but something about Annie put her at ease.

"Annie, can I ask you something? Did Uncle Charlie Joe ever mention his life before he came to Prairie Rose?"

"Never. And in a town this size, that's unusual." Annie refilled Jackie's coffee. "Most folks share at least some stories about where they came from. Charlie Joe would deflect questions, change the subject, talk about anything except his past. Though he would occasionally speak of his family. His niece who was a top-notch lawyer in Austin and his niece who quit teaching to care for her daughter. He was proud of you both."

"Oh, wow, I didn't know that. So did people speculate about other parts of his life?"

"Of course. Some thought he was in witness protection. Others figured he was running from a bad marriage or family troubles, especially since we never saw any family around." Annie's voice grew thoughtful. "But whatever it was, he'd been running long enough to be very good at staying hidden."

"Until now."

"Until now," Annie agreed. "You girls are stirring up attention just by existing here."

Jackie finished her coffee and prepared to leave, but Annie stopped her with a gentle hand on her arm.

"Jackie, I want you to know that this town looks after its own. Charlie Joe became one of us the day he started feeding people and asking nothing in return. That makes you family too."

"Thank you. That means more than you know."

"If you need anything, and I mean *anything*, call me." Annie handed her a business card. "My husband's got connections in county government, my brother's a state trooper, and my cousin runs a security company in Austin. Small town doesn't mean powerless."

After leaving Annie's, she finally made it to the hardware store for the part of the ice machine. Thankfully that was a quick stop.

With her errands done, there was one more piece of business that Jackie wanted to do before she headed back to the restaurant. She decided it was time for a direct conversation with Dr. Thorne.

She found him at his clinic, a small building on Main Street that served the medical needs of Prairie Rose and the surrounding ranching community.

Being a small practice, she could see him in his private office. The doctor looked up from his paperwork with the expression of someone who'd been dreading this conversation for months. He waved her back.

"Dr. Thorne, I'd like to talk to you about Uncle Charlie Joe's death."

"Ms. Prescott. I wondered when you'd come by."

"You've been expecting me?"

"I've been expecting someone to ask the questions you're going to ask." Dr. Thorne gestured to a chair across from his desk. "Questions I've been asking myself every day since Charlie Joe died."

"What questions are those?"

"Whether I did the right thing. Whether I made the right medical decisions. Whether I let personal considerations influence professional judgment." Dr. Thorne removed his glasses and rubbed his eyes. "Whether Charlie Joe would still be alive if I'd been more thorough."

"Tell me about the night he died," Jackie said.

"I got the call from Jovie just after five in the morning. She'd found Charlie Joe slumped over his desk, clearly deceased. When I arrived, all the visible symptoms were consistent with cardiac arrest: skin color, body position, lack of obvious trauma."

"But?"

"But something felt wrong from the moment I walked into that office." Dr. Thorne leaned back in his chair. "Charlie Joe looked... too peaceful. Cardiac arrest usually involves some struggle, some indication of distress. Charlie Joe looked like he'd just fallen asleep."

"Did you mention that to anyone?"

"I mentioned it to Sheriff Henderson, but he was eager to close the case quickly. He said natural deaths were simpler for everyone involved, especially when the deceased was elderly and had known health issues."

"And you agreed with that assessment?"

"Dr. Thorne was quiet for a long moment. "I agreed because I wanted to spare Charlie Joe's family the trauma and expense of an investigation that would probably reach the same conclusion. Cardiac arrest in a seventy-three-year-old man with stress-related chest pains is not unusual."

"But you had doubts," Jackie pressed.

"I had doubts, but I convinced myself they were just... professional anxiety. The uncertainty that comes with making difficult decisions in small town medicine where you don't have access to full diagnostic resources." Dr. Thorne's voice grew smaller. "I told myself I was protecting the family from unnecessary pain and the town by not bringing bad press. A murder in a small town is media gold."

"When did you start regretting that decision?"

"About two weeks after the funeral, when people started asking questions about Charlie Joe's past, when strangers started showing up in town wanting to know about his business dealings." Dr. Thorne looked directly at Jackie. "That's when I realized Charlie Joe's death might not have been as simple as I'd determined."

"Why didn't you reopen the investigation then?"

"So many reasons," he said looking right at Jackie. "Because Sheriff Henderson had already retired and left town. Because the body had been cremated. Because I had no concrete evidence, just a growing feeling that I'd made a terrible, terrible mistake." Dr. Thorne's voice was heavy with guilt. "And because admitting I'd been wrong would have meant acknowledging that I might have helped cover up a murder."

"Do you think Uncle Charlie Joe was murdered?" Jackie asked directly.

"I think Charlie Joe Wagner was a man with dangerous secrets who died under circumstances that should have been investigated more thoroughly. I think my desire to protect his family from additional trauma may have prevented justice from being served." Dr. Thorne met her eyes. "And I think if he was murdered, then my medical assessment helped his killers get away with it."

"What would you do differently if you could go back?"

"I'd insist on an autopsy regardless of the apparent cause of death. I'd document every inconsistency, every detail that didn't fit the cardiac arrest diagnosis. I'd involve state medical authorities instead of relying on my own judgment." Dr. Thorne's voice grew firm. "I'd choose thorough investigation over convenient conclusions and I wouldn't let law enforcement officials pressure me to rush to a conclusion that I knew wasn't right."

"It's not too late," Jackie said.

"What do you mean?"

"I mean if Uncle Charlie Joe was murdered, the people responsible are still out there. Still dangerous. Your medical expertise could still help bring them to justice."

Dr. Thorne considered this. "What do you need from me?"

"A detailed report of everything you observed the morning you examined Uncle Charlie Joe. Every inconsistency, every detail that bothered you, everything you wish you'd investigated more thoroughly."

"And if that report suggests murder?" he asked.

"Then we take it to authorities who are better equipped to handle murder investigations than a small town doctor trying to protect a family he'd never met and his nieces who are just trying to figure out how to run his restaurant and keep his legacy going."

As Jackie walked back to her car, she noticed other people watching her with friendly interest rather than suspicion. The pharmacist waved from his doorway. The librarian smiled through her window. The mechanic at the garage nodded in recognition.

This was her first time in town since taking over the business. It made her realize, Uncle Charlie Joe hadn't just found a place to hide in Prairie Rose. He'd found a community that would protect him. And now they were protecting his family too.

But as she drove back to the restaurant, Jackie couldn't shake the feeling that they were going to need all the protection they could get. The investigation into Uncle Charlie Joe's past was more extensive and organized than she'd realized. Someone with significant resources was very determined to find whatever Uncle Charlie Joe had been hiding.

Back at the restaurant, she found Lauren and Melody examining what appeared to be architectural drawings spread across three tables.

"How was your shopping trip?" Lauren asked.

"Educational. And concerning." Jackie set down the supplies and told them about her conversations in town.

"Private investigators," Lauren said quietly. "That's serious."

"Six different inquiries about our property," Melody added, making notes. "That suggests coordinated effort rather than random interest."

"The good news is that the town's on our side," Jackie said. "Uncle Charlie Joe built real relationships here which we sort of knew, but I confirmed it. People are looking out for us and if Dr. Thorne writes that statement, it might be enough to convict someone and find the killer."

"The bad news is that we're apparently the subject of professional surveillance," Lauren said.

"Which means," Melody concluded, "that whatever Uncle Charlie Joe was hiding is valuable enough to justify significant expense in finding it."

"It also means that all this stuff Tom has been saying about Charlie Joe not fitting in isn't true," Jackie said.

"We knew that though," Lauren laughed.

"Yes, we did."

They spent the rest of the afternoon discussing their options while preparing for the dinner service. By the time they locked up, Jackie had made a decision.

"We really do need to accelerate our timeline," she said as they climbed the stairs to the apartment.

"But how? The restaurant takes up so much of our time," Lauren said.

"I know, but I'm not sure how much longer these people will wait," Jackie replied. "Whatever Uncle Charlie Joe was protecting, other people are closing in on it fast. If we're going to control how this story ends, we need to know what we're dealing with."

"And if what we find is dangerous?" Lauren pressed.

"Then we decide together whether to run or fight." Jackie looked at her sister and niece, thinking about Annie Rigby-Blake's offer of help and Bill Thorne's stories of Uncle Charlie Joe's generosity. "But we decide as a family, and we decide based on the truth instead of fear."

She just hoped it would be enough to protect them from whatever they were about to uncover.

"I know just where we should start," Melody said in her matter-of-fact tone.

Chapter Seventeen

A few days later, Dr. Thorne appeared at the restaurant during their afternoon lull, carrying a thick manila folder and wearing the expression of someone who'd finally decided to unburden himself completely. His usually neat appearance was disheveled with his shirt wrinkled, his hair uncombed, and dark circles under his eyes suggested he hadn't been sleeping well.

"I've prepared the report you asked for," he said, setting the folder on their table with hands that trembled slightly. "Everything I observed, everything I should have investigated, everything I've been regretting for months."

Jackie opened the folder to find pages of detailed medical observations, sketches of the crime scene, and a timeline of Dr. Thorne's decision-making process. The handwriting was meticulous, almost obsessively detailed, as if he'd been trying to document every moment of that terrible morning.

"This is incredibly thorough," she said, scanning the documents. Each page was filled with medical terminology, measurements, observations that painted a picture far more complex than the simple "heart attack" diagnosis they'd been given.

"It's what I should have done six months ago." Dr. Thorne sat down heavily, his shoulders sagging with the weight of months of guilt. "But there's more I need to tell you. About why I was so eager to avoid an autopsy, why I convinced myself Charlie Joe's death was natural causes when my medical training was telling me otherwise."

He paused, staring at his hands. "I've been a coward, and that cowardice may have helped murderers escape justice."

"What do you mean?" Lauren asked gently, sensing the man's genuine anguish.

"I mean I was being pressured by people who had reasons to want Charlie Joe's death handled quietly and quickly." Dr. Thorne's voice grew stronger as he finally told the truth, as if confession was giving him back some of his professional dignity. "Sheriff Henderson made it very clear that he wanted this case closed without complications. He said too much investigation would be bad for the community, bad for tourism, bad for everyone involved."

"Henderson pressured you to avoid an autopsy?" Jackie asked, her lawyer instincts immediately recognizing the legal implications.

"More than pressured. He threatened me." Dr. Thorne's hands clenched into fists on the table. "He suggested that requesting an autopsy would raise questions about my competence as a physician, that it might lead to state medical board reviews of my other decisions. He said the community was already skeptical of having such a young doctor, and that causing unnecessary complications could destroy my career before it really started."

He looked up at them with haunted eyes. "The threat of professional investigation was... effective. My family has been a part of this town for generations. The Thornes were founding families, and I couldn't bring shame to them. I couldn't be the Thorne who destroyed the family reputation."

"So, you chose your career over the truth," Melody said, not judgmentally, but with her characteristic directness.

"I told myself I was choosing the community's peace of mind over unnecessary trauma," Dr. Thorne replied. "I convinced myself that Charlie Joe was old, that he'd been having chest pains, that cardiac arrest was the most logical explanation. I ignored my medical training and followed Henderson's lead because it was easier than fighting."

"Henderson was part of the conspiracy," Melody realized.

"I don't know how deep his involvement went, but he definitely wanted Charlie Joe's death handled as quietly as possible." Dr. Thorne pulled out another document from the folder. It was a timeline he'd created showing Henderson's other suspicious decisions. "After you asked me to review my decisions, I did some research into Henderson's other cases. There's a pattern of suspicious deaths being handled without thorough investigation."

"How many suspicious deaths?" Lauren asked, though her voice suggested she wasn't sure she wanted to know the answer.

"Four over the past fifteen years. All elderly, all ruled natural causes, all involving people who had conflicts with local business interests." Dr. Thorne's voice grew grim as he recited what he'd discovered. "Mrs. Eleanor Vasquez, who was fighting the county's eminent domain claim on her ranch. Mr. Robert Thompson, who was threatening to expose corruption in the local bank. Ms. Sarah Williams, who was documenting illegal dumping by several local businesses. And Mr. James Murphy, who was investigating irregularities in county tax assessments."

"All handled by you?" Jackie asked.

"All handled by me, under pressure from Henderson to avoid complications." Dr. Thorne met her eyes directly. "I see the pattern now that I was too scared or too naïve to see then. Henderson would arrive at the scene before I did, would have already formed his opinion about the cause of death, and would make it clear that agreeing with his assessment was the path of least resistance."

"You think Henderson was using you to cover up multiple murders?" Jackie asked.

"I think Henderson was lazy and corrupt, but I also think he understood that a young doctor trying to establish himself in a small community would be vulnerable to pressure about professional reputation and competence." Dr. Thorne's voice grew stronger, more certain. "And I think I was too focused on protecting my career and my family's reputation to properly protect my patients."

"You were being manipulated," Lauren said with surprising gentleness. "Henderson was exploiting your inexperience and your legitimate concerns about your career."

"That doesn't excuse what I did," Dr. Thorne replied firmly. "I took an oath to do no harm, to seek truth, to protect those who couldn't protect themselves. I failed in all of those obligations."

"But you're willing to make it right now," Jackie said quickly.

"I'm willing to provide whatever medical expertise is needed to bring Charlie Joe's killers to justice, even if it means acknowledging my professional failures publicly." Dr. Thorne's voice grew determined, more like the confident physician he should have been six months ago. "I became a doctor to help people, not to cover up crimes. It's time I remembered that."

"What's in this report that could help our investigation?" Melody asked, flipping through the pages of detailed observations.

"Evidence that Charlie Joe was drugged before he died." Dr. Thorne leaned forward, his medical training finally taking precedence over his fear. "I noticed pupil dilation inconsistent with cardiac arrest. His pupils were constricted, not dilated, which suggests opioid involvement. His body positioning suggested he'd been moved after death as rigor mortis patterns didn't match the position where he was found. And there were skin discoloration patterns that didn't match natural cardiac failure."

He pointed to specific sections of his report, which included detailed sketches and measurements. "I also documented the chemical smell in his office that I dismissed as medication at the time but now realize it was probably from whatever drug was used to incapacitate him. It was sweet, almost medicinal, but not like any heart medication I'm familiar with."

"This is evidence of murder," Jackie said, feeling both vindicated and horrified.

"This is evidence that I should have recognized as murder months ago," Dr. Thorne corrected, his voice heavy with self-recrimination. "But yes, it strongly suggests Charlie Joe was poisoned with something that caused cardiac symptoms while leaving him conscious long enough to be positioned at his desk."

He pulled out another set of documents. "I've also included toxicology protocols that should have been followed, evidence collection procedures that were ignored, and timeline inconsistencies that I noticed but didn't pursue."

"Can you testify to this?" Lauren asked.

"I can and will testify to everything in that report. I can also provide expert testimony about how the investigation should have been conducted and what evidence was lost due to my failure to insist on proper procedures." Dr. Thorne stood up, looking more confident than he had since they met him. "I'll face whatever professional consequences come from this, but I won't let fear silence me again."

He paused at the door, turning back to face them. "Charlie Joe deserved better medical care in death than I provided. His family deserves the truth about what happened to him. And the community deserves to know that their doctor won't be pressured into covering up crimes anymore."

"Dr. Thorne," Jackie said. "Thank you. This took real courage."

"No," he replied quietly. "Courage would have been doing this six months ago. This is just... overdue honesty. But it's a start."

After he left, the three women sat in silence, processing the weight of what they'd just learned.

"So, Uncle Charlie Joe was definitely murdered," Lauren said finally.

"And there's a pattern of suspicious deaths being covered up," Melody added, consulting her notes.

"And we now have medical evidence that could help convict his killers," Jackie concluded. "Dr. Thorne just gave us everything we need to reopen this case properly."

But as she looked at the detailed medical report, Jackie also felt a deep sadness for Dr. Thorne, a good man who'd made terrible choices under pressure, and who was now trying to find the courage to make amends. It was a reminder that sometimes the people who seemed complicit were actually victims themselves, caught between impossible choices in circumstances they weren't equipped to handle.

"He's going to lose his medical license over this, isn't he?" Lauren asked quietly.

"Maybe," Jackie said. "But he's going to save his soul. And maybe that's worth more than his career."

"Plus, his testimony could prevent other doctors from being pressured the same way," Melody observed. "His willingness to speak out could protect future patients."

As they locked away Dr. Thorne's report in their safe, Jackie realized that Uncle Charlie Joe's murder had created more victims than just Uncle Charlie Joe himself. Dr. Thorne, the community's trust in their institutions, the families of other suspicious death victims. They had all been damaged by the conspiracy they were now trying to unravel.

But they were also discovering that healing was possible, that people could find the courage to do the right thing even when it cost them everything they'd worked for.

<h1 style="text-align:center">Chapter Eighteen</h1>

Since the restaurant was only closed on Mondays, they had to wait until the following one to track the leads. However, before they could head out, they had to start meat in the smokers, but once that was done, they had a few hours before they had to check it again.

They headed into town to start their research at the place that Melody suggested.

The Prairie Rose Public Library was housed in a converted Victorian mansion on the town's main street, complete with wraparound porches and gingerbread trim that made it look more like someone's grandmother's house than a repository of information.

Jackie pushed through the heavy oak doors, followed by Lauren and Melody, each of them carrying notebooks and a sense of urgency that had been building since Sheriff Martinez's visit and more so since Jackie's trip to town the other day.

"Can I help you ladies?" The librarian behind the circulation desk was a woman in her seventies with silver hair pinned up in an elaborate bun and eyes that missed nothing. Her name tag read "Mrs. Dorothy Fitzgerald, Head Librarian."

"We're hoping to research some local history," Jackie said. "Specifically, newspaper from the 1990s."

Mrs. Fitzgerald's eyes lit up with the special enthusiasm that librarians reserved for patrons with actual research projects.

"Those will be in our archives room. We don't get many requests for the archives these days."

Jackie and Lauren exchanged startled glances. "Archives?" Lauren repeated faintly. "The 1990s are considered... archives?"

"Oh yes, dear. Anything older than twenty years gets moved to the historical archive system." Mrs. Fitzgerald smiled kindly. "I know it seems recent to those of us who lived through it, but for research purposes, the nineties are definitely historical now."

"I was in high school in the nineties, at least the early nineties," Jackie said, still looking stunned.

"Yeah, I was just a freshman," Lauren added. "When did we become historical figures?"

"When you stopped paying attention to the passage of time," Melody said dryly. "The 1990s ended about twenty-five years ago. That's a full generation."

"Thank you for that reality check," Jackie muttered.

"We're Charlie Joe Wagner's great-nieces," Lauren explained. "We inherited his restaurant and we're trying to learn more about when he first came to Prairie Rose."

"Ah, I thought you might be, but I didn't want to pry." Mrs. Fitzgerald's expression grew more thoughtful. "Charlie Joe. Now that's a man who valued his privacy. But he also donated generously to our book acquisition fund every year." She gestured toward a comfortable reading area with several computer terminals. "The newspaper archives are digitized back to 1985. What specific years are you interested in?"

"1994 to 1996," Melody said promptly. "We're looking for any mentions of new businesses, new residents, or unusual events during that time period."

Mrs. Fitzgerald led them to the computers and showed them how to navigate the archive system. "I'll leave you to it, but don't hesitate to ask if you need help. And girls?" She paused at the edge of the reading area. "Charlie Joe was a good man. Whatever you're looking for, I hope you find answers that honor his memory."

"We hope so too," Lauren smiled.

They settled at adjacent computers, dividing up the years between them. Jackie took 1994, Lauren focused on 1995, and Melody managed 1996. The Prairie Rose Gazette was a weekly publication, so there were numerous issues to review, but the small-town format meant that everything was covered. From new business licenses, property sales, community events, even minor police incidents, they could search for anything.

"Here's something," Lauren said after twenty minutes of searching. "March 15, 1995: 'New Business Opens on Highway 12.' It's about Uncle Charlie Joe opening the restaurant, but listen to this description: 'The proprietor, Charles Wagner, brings years of culinary experience to Prairie Rose, though he declines to discuss his previous ventures, preferring to focus on serving quality barbecue to his new community.'"

"Even then, people noticed he was secretive about his past," Jackie observed.

"Found the property purchase," Melody announced. "February 3, 1995. 'Wagner Purchases Former Thorne Ranch.' Not from the Whitfields. Uncle Charlie Joe bought the land from the Thorne family for cash ... $57,000 for twelve acres."

"Cash?" Jackie looked up from her screen. "That's unusual for a property purchase that size at that time."

"Very unusual," agreed a voice behind them. They turned to see Mrs. Fitzgerald approaching with a tray of coffee and cookies. "I remember when that sale went through. It caused quite a stir in town because cash sales that large were practically unheard of, well back then. Also, the Whitfield's were not happy about the sale. They wanted that land for themselves."

"Tom doesn't seem old enough to have been involved in that back then," Jackie said.

"You're right. He was still away at college, but his daddy, Dale, was not happy. They had been trying to buy that land from the Thornes, but Charlie Joe came in with a better offer."

That filled in some of the hatred that Tom Whitfield had for them and Charlie Joe.

"Do you remember anything else about when Uncle Charlie Joe arrived?" Lauren asked.

Mrs. Fitzgerald settled into a nearby chair, clearly happy to share her memories. "Oh, I remember quite well. He came into the library his second week in town, wanting to get a library card and donate some books. But he was... cautious. Asked a lot of questions about our patron privacy policies, whether we kept records of what people checked out."

"What did he want to research?" Melody asked.

"Local history, land records, zoning laws. But also..." Mrs. Fitzgerald paused, as if deciding whether to continue. "He spent a lot of time reading old newspapers from other Texas towns. Like he was checking to see if his name appeared anywhere."

Jackie and Lauren exchanged glances. "Did it? Appear anywhere, I mean?"

"Not that I ever saw. But then again, I wasn't looking for anything in particular." Mrs. Fitzgerald sipped her coffee thoughtfully.

"What I did notice was that he seemed relieved every time he finished reading a paper and found nothing."

"Like he was making sure he'd stayed hidden," Jackie said.

"Exactly. And then there was the matter of Ezra Hutchins."

"We know he taught Uncle Charlie Joe about barbecue," Lauren said.

"He did more than that," Mrs. Fitzgerald said. "Ezra came in here a few weeks after Charlie Joe arrived, asking for books about identity documentation, legal name changes, that sort of thing. When I asked if he was thinking of changing his name, he said it was research for a friend."

Melody looked up from her computer. "Uncle Charlie Joe was considering changing his name?"

"Or maybe he'd already changed it once and was thinking about doing it again," Mrs. Fitzgerald suggested. "Ezra was very careful about how he phrased things, but I got the impression this 'friend' needed to know his options."

Jackie found herself leaning forward. "Mrs. Fitzgerald, did anyone else ever come in asking about Uncle Charlie Joe? Recently, I mean?"

The librarian's expression grew wary. "Why do you ask?"

"Because we've had some... unusual interest in our family history lately. People asking questions around town."

"Ah." Mrs. Fitzgerald nodded knowingly. "Yes, there have been several inquiries in the past month. Very polite people, very professional, but asking the kinds of questions that made me uncomfortable."

"What kinds of questions?" Lauren asked.

"Whether Charlie Joe ever used the computers here, what kinds of research he did, if he ever mentioned family or talked about his past. I told them the same thing I tell everyone, we don't discuss our patrons' activities with anyone, for any reason."

"Good for you," Jackie said with feeling.

"Though I will say," Mrs. Fitzgerald continued, "one of them was quite persistent. A woman, very well-dressed, said she was a genealogist helping the family trace their heritage. She had identification that looked official, but something about her didn't sit right with me."

"What didn't sit right?" Melody asked.

"She knew too much. Asked about specific dates, specific events. Genealogists usually start with broad questions and narrow down. This woman came in with a very focused agenda."

Jackie felt a chill. "Do you remember what she looked like?"

"Silver hair, very well put together, probably around my age. Reminded me a bit of that actress … um, you know, the one who played the mother in that legal drama."

"Ruth Pemberton," Lauren said quietly looking directly at Jackie.

Mrs. Fitzgerald nodded. "That was the name she gave. Said she was a distant relative working on the family tree."

"She's not part of our family, but we have met her," Jackie said. She left off the part about getting a text message after her visit.

"I wish we knew more about her," Lauren said.

Jackie's laptop chimed with a search result. "I found something," she said, scanning the screen. "June 1994, from the Austin Business Journal online archive. 'Richardson Financial Partners Under Investigation.' Listen to this: 'Federal authorities are investigating Richardson Financial Partners following allegations of investment fraud. Senior partner Gerald Pemberton was arrested yesterday, while junior partner Charles Joseph Wagner remains missing. Investigators believe Wagner may have fled the country with client funds estimated at over forty million dollars.'"

"So, Uncle Charlie Joe was already on the run a full year before he came to Prairie Rose," Lauren said.

"Which means he spent a year somewhere else first," Melody added. "The question is where, and why did he move again?"

Jackie continued reading. "There's more. 'Wagner's whereabouts remain unknown, though sources close to the investigation suggest he may have been cooperating with federal authorities before his disappearance. A key witness in the case, accounting consultant Matt Klein, died in a single-car accident two days before Wagner vanished.'"

"Matt Klein," Lauren repeated. "Where have I heard that name?"

Melody's fingers flew across her keyboard. "Matt Klein, local wedding and event planner, established his business in Prairie Rose in 1996. One year after Uncle Charlie Joe arrived."

Mrs. Fitzgerald had gone very still. "Matt Klein has been planning events here for almost thirty years. He organized the library's fundraising gala just last month."

"Has he ever asked about Uncle Charlie Joe?" Lauren asked.

"Not directly. But now that you mention it..." Mrs. Fitzgerald's brow furrowed in concentration. "He volunteered to help with our local history digitization project a few years ago. Spent a lot of time going through old records, said he was interested in documenting the town's business development."

"What kind of records?" Jackie asked.

"Property transfers, business licenses, building permits. All public information, but Matt was very thorough. Very interested in who arrived when and from where."

Jackie felt pieces of the puzzle shifting into new configurations. "So, we have Uncle Charlie Joe arriving in 1995, running from fraud charges and a murdered witness. We have Matt Klein, who shares a unique name with the dead witness, arriving in 1996. And we have Ruth Pemberton, whose name connects to Uncle Charlie Joe's former business partner, asking questions about Uncle Charlie Joe's activities."

"That's a lot of coincidences," Lauren said.

"No such thing as coincidences in investigations," Melody said matter-of-factly. "Only patterns that haven't been properly analyzed yet."

"I think I should make some phone calls," Mrs. Fitzgerald said, standing up. "There are a few people in town who might remember more details about those early years."

As the librarian walked away, Jackie turned back to her computer with renewed focus. "We need to find out what happened during that missing year. Where was Uncle Charlie Joe between when he disappeared from Austin and when he showed up here?"

"And we need to figure out if Matt Klein is really the same person as the murdered witness, or if someone is using his identity," Lauren added.

"And we need to understand what Ruth Pemberton really wants," Melody said. "Because if she's connected to Gerald Pemberton, she might know things about Uncle Charlie Joe's evidence that we don't."

They spent the next two hours digging deeper into the archives, searching for any mention of the names connected to their mystery. What they found painted a picture of a small town that had unknowingly become a refuge for people running from dangerous pasts.

"Look at this," Lauren said, pointing to her screen. "August 1995: 'Local Resident Provides Anonymous Tip Leading to Drug Bust.' Someone with inside knowledge helped the sheriff's department intercept a major drug shipment passing through Prairie Rose."

"And this," Jackie added. "October 1995: 'Fire at Abandoned Warehouse Reveals Hidden Documents.' The fire department found evidence of illegal activity when they responded to a suspicious fire at an old building on the outskirts of town."

"Someone was cleaning house," Melody noted. "Removing evidence, eliminating connections."

"Uncle Charlie Joe," Lauren said quietly. "He was helping law enforcement while staying hidden himself."

Mrs. Fitzgerald returned with a small group of elderly residents, all of whom looked excited to be part of a historical research project.

"These folks remember the mid-90s very well," she announced. "They have some interesting stories about the people who arrived in Prairie Rose during that time."

"There were more people than just Uncle Charlie Joe?" Jackie asked.

"Oh yes," said a man who Jackie recognized as Bill Thorne from the general store and the same family that had sold Uncle Charlie Joe his land. "That was quite a year for newcomers. We had Charlie Joe, of course, and Matt Klein arrived about six months or so later. Then there was that woman who opened the antique shop, and the fellow who started the computer repair business."

"All within about eighteen months," added a woman named Alice Morrison. "We joked that Prairie Rose was becoming a regular boomtown."

"Did any of them know each other?" Lauren asked.

"Well, that's the funny thing," Bill said. "They all seemed to avoid each other, at least at first. Charlie Joe was friendly with everyone, but he never seemed to recognize any of the other newcomers. And they didn't seem to recognize him either."

"But you thought they should have?" Melody asked.

"Just had the feeling that maybe they'd all come from the same place, you know? Similar way of talking, similar habits. Charlie Joe and Matt both asked a lot of questions about local law enforcement when they first arrived."

"What kinds of questions?" Jackie asked.

"How long Sheriff Henderson had been in office, whether he was honest, whether the department had good relationships with state and federal agencies." Alice's expression grew thoughtful. "Looking back, it seemed like they were all trying to figure out if Prairie Rose was a safe place to settle down."

"A safe place to hide," Lauren murmured.

"And maybe they were all hiding from the same thing," Jackie added.

"Well thank you all. We have to get back to the restaurant to check on the smoker, but we really appreciate your time," Lauren said, looking around at all the friendly faces.

"We hope it helps. We all liked Charlie Joe, and we miss him around here," Bill said for the group.

As they gathered their notes and prepared to leave the library, Mrs. Fitzgerald pulled Jackie aside.

"I probably shouldn't tell you this," she said quietly, "but Matt Klein called this morning. Asked if anyone had been in looking at old records lately. I told him we don't discuss patron activities, but..." She paused. "Be careful, dear. I've lived in Prairie Rose for seventy years, and I've learned to trust my instincts about people. Something about this whole situation feels dangerous."

"Thank you for that and for your help with all of this."

Walking back to their car, Jackie couldn't shake the feeling that they were being watched. The late afternoon sun cast long shadows between the buildings, and every movement in her peripheral vision made her tense.

"We're getting close to something," she said to Lauren and Melody. "And I think people are starting to notice."

"The question is," Lauren replied, "are we getting close to the truth, or are we getting close to trouble?"

"Both," Melody said with certainty. "Uncle Charlie Joe's story is more complicated than we thought. And we're not the only ones trying to piece it together."

As they drove back to the restaurant, Jackie realized that their investigation had revealed as many new questions as answers. But it had also revealed something else: Uncle Charlie Joe hadn't been the only person who'd found refuge in Prairie Rose. The small town had been a haven for people running from dangerous situations.

The question now was whether it could continue to protect them, or whether the past was finally catching up to everyone who'd thought they could hide in the Hill Country forever.

Chapter Nineteen

After their disturbing discoveries at the library about Matt Klein's connection to the Richardson Financial case, Jackie knew they couldn't wait any longer. They needed answers about the man who had been quietly operating an event planning business in their town for nearly thirty years.

"I still think this is risky," Lauren said as they walked across the town square toward Klein Events & Planning. "If he's connected to Uncle Charlie Joe's past, we don't know which side he was on."

"That's exactly why we need to talk to him," Jackie replied. "We can't keep operating in the dark when people are threatening us."

Melody consulted her notebook. "Based on the timeline, Matt Klein arrived in Prairie Rose approximately six months after Uncle Charlie Joe. If he's the same person who was supposed to testify in the Richardson Financial case, that's not a coincidence."

Klein Events & Planning occupied a small storefront between the hardware store and the antique shop. Through the window, they could see a man in his late sixties arranging flowers with practiced precision. When they entered, he looked up with an expression that immediately shifted from professional courtesy to something that looked like relief.

"You must be Charlie Joe's great-nieces," he said, setting down his work. "I've been hoping you'd come see me. I'm Matt Klein."

Jackie studied his face carefully. "You've been hoping we'd come?"

"For weeks now. Ever since I heard about the threats you've been receiving."

"You heard about those?" Jackie asked.

"Yes, I'm sure you understand by now how a small town works." Matt moved to the front door and flipped the sign to 'Closed.' "We need to talk, but not here. Too many windows."

He led them to his back office, but instead of settling behind his desk, he opened a filing cabinet and withdrew a thick folder and what appeared to be a federal communication device.

"Before we go any further," he said, "I need you to know that I've been in contact with FBI Financial Crimes Division for the past fifteen years. And Charles... err ... Charlie Joe was working with us too. I knew him as Charles back then. He took up the Charlie Joe when he moved here. Didn't use his last name often either. He thought it would help him blend in."

The words hung in the air like a revelation that changed everything.

"Why did you keep your name? Wouldn't someone find out who you were?"

"My name is fairly plain, almost common. Plus, back in the early 90s, there weren't cameras on every corner. No Facebook, no Instagram. You could hide in plain sight, and nobody would blink an eye, especially when they think you're dead."

"You said he was working with you. Working with you how?" Lauren asked.

"Your uncle wasn't hiding from the law," Matt said, his voice growing stronger. "He was helping us build a case against the real criminals behind Richardson Financial. People who had so much power and so many connections that it took us three decades to finally get close to bringing them down."

"You're saying Uncle Charlie Joe was innocent?" Jackie felt her worldview shifting.

"Completely innocent. Charles stumbled onto the money laundering operation by accident when he was doing routine financial analysis. When he tried to report it through normal channels, he discovered the corruption went much deeper than anyone realized."

Matt opened the folder, revealing hundreds of pages of documents, photographs, and what appeared to be surveillance reports. "Gerald Pemberton wasn't the mastermind. He was middle management. The real power behind Richardson Financial was someone much more dangerous."

"Who?" Melody asked, leaning forward.

"Harrison Kale."

Jackie felt ice form in her stomach. "The developer who's been pressuring us to sell?"

"Kale's development company is a front for one of the largest money laundering operations in the Southwest. Richardson Financial was just one of dozens of legitimate businesses he used to clean dirty money." Matt's expression grew grim. "When Charles discovered the connection, Kale ordered him eliminated."

"But Uncle Charlie Joe escaped," Lauren said.

"With our help. I was FBI Financial Crimes, working undercover as an accounting consultant. When we realized Charles had stumbled onto something huge, we staged my death and helped both of us disappear."

"You're FBI?" Jackie asked.

"Was FBI. I'm officially retired now, but I've been working this case for thirty years." Matt pulled out his credentials. The name read Special Agent Matthew Klein. "Charles Wagner was our most valuable asset in building a case against Kale's organization."

"Then why didn't you arrest Kale years ago?" Melody asked.

"Because he's smart, careful, and has connections in law enforcement, politics, and financial institutions across multiple states. We needed ironclad evidence, and we needed to identify all the players in his network before we moved." Matt's voice grew sad. "Charles spent thirty years documenting everything, gathering proof, waiting for the right moment to surface."

"What changed?" Lauren asked.

"Kale's getting desperate. New federal banking regulations are making it harder to launder money through real estate transactions. He needs to liquidate assets quickly, which is why he's been so aggressive about acquiring your property."

"It's not just about the land," Jackie realized.

"It's about what's under the land. Charles's final evidence cache is buried on your property. Financial records, recorded conversations, proof of murders. Everything we need to bring down Kale's entire operation."

"What? How …?" Lauren couldn't quite form the question she wanted to ask.

"I helped him hide it," Matt said. "We have been working together all along, but we had to keep our distance and most of the time we did. Meeting in secret."

"Okay, so you said that Kale is the mastermind and that Pemberton was the only one charged. Do you know anything about Ruth Pemberton who is here in town asking questions about Charlie Joe?"

"That's his sister but she's just a pawn in Harrison Kale's plan. He keeps telling her that if she helps him, he'll get her brother released. She came to see me recently to confess everything. We now have her in protective custody."

"Wow, just wow." Jackie and Lauren were flabbergasted.

"I did not expect that."

"Okay, one more question. There were two other people who moved to town around the same time as you and Uncle Charlie Joe, did you know them? Are they part of this?" Lauren asked.

"No, just coincidence, but I thought at first they might have been working with Kale. They have since been cleared." Matt smiled. "Anything else?"

"No, that answers all my questions, at least currently." Jackie looked at Lauren and Melody. They both nodded.

Matt stood up and walked to a wall safe, withdrawing a small device that looked like a satellite phone. "I've been waiting for authorization to move against Kale. That authorization came through an hour ago."

"What does that mean?" Lauren asked.

"It means we're done hiding. Tonight, we're going to give Kale exactly what he wants, a chance to retrieve Charlie Joe's evidence. And when he shows up to get it, we'll be ready."

"You want to use us as bait," Jackie said.

"I want to finish what Charlie Joe started. He spent thirty years of his life building this case, and he died before he could see justice done. But he left us everything we need to complete his work."

Matt activated the device, and within moments, a woman's voice crackled through: "Agent Klein, this is Director Lowen. You have full authorization for Operation Longhorn. Assets are in position."

"Copy that, Director. The family is on board."

"Wait," Jackie said. "We haven't agreed to anything yet."

Matt looked at each of them carefully. "Charles believed in you. He believed you were strong enough to finish what he started, brave enough to stand up to people who've been operating with impunity for decades."

"What exactly are you asking us to do?" Lauren asked.

"Exactly what you've been doing. Run your restaurant, live your lives, but tomorrow night, when Kale comes for the evidence, we'll be ready for him." Matt's expression grew determined. "Thirty years is long enough for killers to run free."

"How do you know he will come tomorrow?"

"We have surveillance all over town. We also have an insider working with him. The plan at current is for Kale to confront y'all tomorrow after hours."

"And if something goes wrong?" Melody asked.

"Then we'll have FBI agents, state police, and federal marshals backing us up. Kale's going to walk into the most thorough law enforcement operation in Texas history."

Jackie looked at Lauren and Melody, seeing her own determination reflected in their faces. They'd inherited more than a restaurant from Uncle Charlie Joe. They'd inherited his fight for justice.

"Will we be wearing wires?" Lauren asked.

"Better than that. This entire town will be under surveillance. Every move Kale makes, every word he says, every person he contacts, we'll have it all documented."

As Matt explained the details of the operation, Jackie realized that Uncle Charlie Joe's story was finally reaching its conclusion. Not with hiding and running, but with standing up and fighting back.

Now that they knew the truth, Jackie also felt compelled to address their earlier suspicions.

"Matt, we need to tell you something. We suspected Jovie of being involved in Uncle Charlie Joe's death."

"Jovie?" Matt looked genuinely surprised. "Why?"

"She'd been embezzling money to pay for her daughter's medical bills. We thought maybe Uncle Charlie Joe found out and threatened to expose her."

Matt shook his head. "Charles knew about the money. He told me about it months ago."

"He knew?" Lauren asked.

"He was planning to forgive the debt and give her a bonus to cover the rest of her daughter's treatments. He said Jovie had been more loyal to him than his own family." Matt's expression grew sad. "In fact, one of the reasons he was so determined to leave the restaurant to you girls was because he wanted to make sure Jovie would be taken care of. He knew you'd need her expertise and hoped you'd treat her fairly."

"We accused her of murder," Jackie said, feeling sick with guilt. "Jovie's been protecting his legacy, not destroying it. She could have sold information about his routines, his security measures, his hiding places to Kale's people. Instead, she's been trying to keep the restaurant running exactly the way Uncle Charlie Joe would have wanted."

"We need to apologize," Lauren said immediately.

"We need to make this right," Jackie agreed.

"Matt, also, we need to discuss Tom Whitfield."

"The neighbor?" Matt asked.

"The neighbor who's been systematically harassing us, who had a thirty-year grudge against Uncle Charlie Joe, and who seems to know an awful lot about what happened the night he died."

Jackie pulled out her notebook where she'd been documenting Tom's escalating campaign of harassment. "Tom told us his family has been trying to buy our land for four generations. He believes Uncle Charlie Joe stole it from them with a suspicious cash purchase. He's been sabotaging our business in increasingly sophisticated ways."

"I hadn't heard this, just Kale's threats. What kinds of sabotage?" Matt asked.

"Cattle in our parking lot, misdirected deliveries, severed phone lines, contaminated water supply. All just barely legal, all designed to make our business fail so we'll be forced to sell to him at below market prices."

"That's harassment, not murder," Matt pointed out.

"But he also knew Uncle Charlie Joe was scared those final months," Lauren added. "He told us Charlie Joe was acting paranoid, checking locks, looking over his shoulder. How would Tom know that unless he was watching him closely?"

"Very closely," Melody said, consulting her own notes. "Tom mentioned specific details about Uncle Charlie Joe's behavior, his routines, his security measures. That level of surveillance suggests obsessive interest."

"Plus, Tom made several statements that could be interpreted as threats," Jackie continued. "He said Prairie Rose doesn't take kindly to outsiders who don't respect established ways. He said Charlie Joe never learned that lesson. He said sometimes accidents happen to isolated folks who don't have strong community connections."

Matt frowned. "Those do sound threatening. But do you have any evidence connecting Tom to Charlie Joe's actual death?"

"Opportunity," Melody said. "Tom knows our property intimately. He's demonstrated the ability to move around on it without being detected. He could have accessed Uncle Charlie Joe's routine and location easily."

"Means," Lauren added. "Tom carries a knife, owns firearms, and would know how to make a death look natural. Plus, as a rancher, he'd have access to veterinary drugs that could cause heart attacks."

"And motive," Jackie concluded. "Tom believes Uncle Charlie Joe stole his family's land. He's spent three decades trying to get it back. He's demonstrated he'll use increasingly aggressive tactics when peaceful methods fail."

Matt was quiet for a long moment, processing this information. "Have you considered that Tom might be working with the real killers? That he might be their local asset, the person who provided intelligence about Charlie Joe's routines and security measures?"

"You think Tom was involved in the larger conspiracy?" Jackie asked.

"I think thirty years of systematic surveillance and harassment doesn't develop overnight. Tom's campaign against your family is too sophisticated, too well-coordinated to be purely personal." Matt pulled out a map of the area. "Look at your property's location. It's isolated, surrounded by Tom's land, with multiple access points that Tom would know intimately."

"Perfect for surveillance," Melody realized.

"And perfect for eliminating someone who needed to be silenced," Matt added grimly. "Charlie Joe was getting close to surfacing with his evidence. Someone with local knowledge would have been invaluable for planning his elimination."

"So, Tom killed Uncle Charlie Joe on behalf of the larger conspiracy?" Lauren asked.

"Or Tom provided the intelligence that allowed the larger conspiracy to kill Charlie Joe effectively," Matt corrected. "Either way, he's involved in murder, not just harassment."

Jackie felt the pieces clicking into place. "That's why Tom's harassment campaign has been so sophisticated. He's not just a greedy neighbor. He's a criminal operative who's been working to cover up evidence of Uncle Charlie Joe's murder."

"And now he's trying to force us off the property before we can discover what Uncle Charlie Joe was hiding," Lauren added.

"We need to be very careful," Matt warned. "If Tom is involved in this conspiracy, he's dangerous in ways we haven't fully appreciated. This isn't just about land disputes anymore."

As they prepared to leave, Matt stopped them. "One more thing, Charlie Joe wanted me to tell you something if this day ever came. He said to remember that courage isn't the absence of fear. It's doing what's right despite the fear."

"That sounds like him," Lauren said softly.

"And he said to tell you that he was proud of the family you'd become, even before you knew it yourselves."

As they walked back across the town square, Jackie felt a strange sense of completion. Uncle Charlie Joe hadn't just left them a restaurant and a mystery to solve. He'd left them the chance to be part of something larger than themselves, something that would protect other families from the kind of criminals who destroyed lives for profit.

"Are we really doing this?" Lauren asked.

"We're really doing this," Jackie replied. "For Uncle Charlie Joe, for all the people Kale has hurt, and for each other."

"And because," Melody added with her characteristic precision, "the statistical probability of success is significantly higher when law enforcement has thirty years to prepare."

Jackie laughed. "You are so right, Melody."

That evening, as they went through their usual closing routine, Jackie noticed the subtle signs that they weren't alone. A van parked at the edge of the property that hadn't been there before. Unfamiliar faces in the distance who seemed to be watching the restaurant. The quiet efficiency of professionals setting up for an operation.

Matt had explained they would start getting equipment in place the day before so that they could be nearly invisible when Kale and his men showed up.

But inside the restaurant, everything felt normal. Lauren counted receipts, Melody updated inventory, Jovie cleaned equipment. The ordinary rhythm of their life continued, even as they prepared for an extraordinary confrontation.

"Whatever happens tomorrow," Jackie said as they climbed the stairs to their apartment, "we face it together."

"Together," Lauren agreed.

"As a family," Melody added.

And for the first time since inheriting Charlie Joe's BBQ Shack, Jackie felt like they were finally living up to Uncle Charlie Joe's faith in them.

Chapter Twenty

They found Jovie in the kitchen at 5 AM, starting the morning prep as she had every day for the past weeks. When she saw them, her face was guarded and tired.

"Jovie," Jackie began, "we owe you an enormous apology."

"You don't owe me anything," Jovie said quietly. "I stole from Charlie Joe. You had every right to suspect me."

"We didn't have the right to accuse you of murder without knowing all the facts," Lauren said firmly. "That was wrong."

"Uncle Charlie Joe knew about the money," Melody added. "Matt Klein told us. Uncle Charlie Joe was planning to forgive the debt."

Jovie's hands stilled on the brisket she'd been trimming. "He knew?"

"He knew, and he understood," Jackie said. "He was planning to give you a bonus to cover your daughter's remaining medical expenses."

"And he specifically told Matt that he hoped we'd treat you fairly, that you'd been more loyal to him than his own family," Lauren added. "Which is all true. We weren't there for him. You were."

Jovie set down her knife and turned to face them, tears streaming down her face. "I've felt so guilty, taking that money. Every day, thinking about how disappointed he'd be if he knew."

"He wasn't disappointed," Jackie said gently. "He was proud of you for taking care of your daughter."

"He said that family always comes first," Lauren added. "And you were family to him."

"Can you forgive us for doubting you?" Jackie asked.

"Can you forgive me for stealing?" Jovie countered.

"There's nothing to forgive," Lauren said. "You were protecting your family. Uncle Charlie Joe understood that. We understand that now too."

Jovie nodded, wiping her eyes. "So, what do we do now?"

"Now we work together to finish what Uncle Charlie Joe started," Jackie said reaching a hand towards Jovie and one to Lauren. "All of us. As family."

"And the money I took?" Jovie asked but not yet taking Jackie's hand.

"Consider it an advance on your salary increase," Lauren said with a smile. "We're going to need you more than ever if we're going to solve this mystery and save this restaurant."

"Plus," Jackie added, "someone who's been loyal enough to keep this place running for two months while grieving and worrying about her daughter's health deserves a raise, not suspicion."

Jovie smiled through her tears, finally taking Jackie's outstretched hand. "Charlie Joe would be proud of the women you've become."

"He'd be proud of all of us," Lauren said. "Now let's go catch the real criminals."

The three women laughed and cried while holding hands. It was a promise, a pact that they were united in this business and this new family, Charlie Joe's BBQ Shack family, by blood and found family.

The confrontation began at 11:26 PM, but not the way Matt Klein had planned.

Jackie, Lauren, and Melody crouched behind the main counter as instructed, listening through their earpieces as FBI agents reported Kale's vehicles approaching. But instead of the controlled entry they'd rehearsed, chaos erupted when Kale's thermal imaging equipment detected the federal agents' positions.

"All units compromised," Matt's voice crackled through their earpieces. "Kale knows we're here. Switching to containment protocol."

The back door exploded inward with a deafening crash. Through the smoke, Harrison Kale's voice cut through the darkness, no longer the smooth businessman but something far more dangerous.

"Very impressive, ladies. Federal surveillance, coordinated response, the whole theatrical production." His footsteps moved methodically through the dining room. "Unfortunately for everyone involved, I came prepared for treachery."

Jackie pressed record on her phone as Matt had instructed, but her hands were shaking. This wasn't going according to plan.

"Where are my federal friends hiding?" Kale continued conversationally. "Don't worry, I won't hurt them. Much. I just need them to understand that I have something they want more than they want me."

A new smell reached Jackie's nose. It was gasoline. Her blood turned to ice.

"You're going to burn the restaurant?" Lauren called out, abandoning their hiding spot as the acrid fumes grew stronger.

"Only if necessary," Kale replied. "You see, I know Charlie Joe's evidence is somewhere on this property. If I can't have it, no one can. But I'd prefer to retrieve it intact."

Through the windows, Jackie could see multiple small fires being lit around the building's perimeter. Kale's associates were creating a fire barrier, trapping everyone inside while giving him leverage over the FBI agents outside.

"The evidence isn't in here," Melody said suddenly, her voice carrying that precise tone she used when stating facts. "Uncle Charlie Joe was too smart to hide important documents in a wooden building."

Kale's flashlight beam swung toward her. "Smart girl. Where is it then?"

Jackie felt her legal training kick in, the same focused clarity she'd used in hundreds of courtroom confrontations. Keep him talking. Make him reveal information. Control the conversation.

"That depends on what you're offering in exchange," she said, standing up slowly with her hands visible. "You want the evidence, and we want safe passage for everyone in this building."

"Negotiating, counselor?" Kale's laugh held no humor. "I'm afraid you don't have much leverage. Outside there are federal agents who can't move without risking everyone inside burning alive. Inside are three women and whatever's left of Charlie Joe's misguided conscience."

"Actually," Jackie said, stepping into the light, "inside is someone who's spent fifteen years negotiating with criminals who thought they held all the cards. What exactly do you think Charlie Joe documented about your operation?"

"Everything," Kale said simply. "Financial records, meeting transcripts, photographs of murders being planned. Thirty years of evidence that would put me and two hundred associates in federal prison for life."

"That's a lot of people who might prefer you didn't get caught," Jackie observed. "How many of them know you're here tonight? How many are wondering if you'll trade their freedom for your own?"

She could see Kale's jaw tighten. Good. She was getting to him.

"Where is the evidence?" he demanded.

"Lauren," Jackie said calmly, never taking her eyes off Kale. "Why don't you explain Charlie Joe's security system to Mr. Kale?"

Lauren understood immediately. While Jackie held Kale's attention, she and Melody needed to reach the real evidence cache before Kale did or at least prevent him from getting to it.

"Charlie Joe was paranoid about electronic surveillance," Lauren said, moving slowly toward the kitchen. "Everything important is stored in physical form, in multiple locations, with backup copies."

"Multiple locations?" Kale's attention sharpened.

"Under the oak tree is just the first cache," Melody added, following her mother toward the back door. "The really damaging evidence is somewhere much more secure."

"Stop," Kale commanded, but Jackie stepped forward, reclaiming his focus.

"You know what's interesting about thirty years of evidence?" she continued. "It's not just financial records. It's murder confessions. Including recorded conversations about killing federal agents."

"What recorded conversations?" Kale's voice had gone deadly quiet.

"The ones where you discuss eliminating FBI Agent Matthew Klein. The conversations Charlie Joe documented before Klein's supposed death." Jackie smiled coldly. "Did you know Klein survived the car crash you arranged? Did you know he's been documenting everything you've done since 1994?"

Kale spun toward the kitchen, realizing too late that Lauren and Melody had used his distraction to slip outside. "Bring them back, or I start shooting."

"They're not going anywhere dangerous," Jackie said quickly. "The evidence isn't something they can destroy or move. It's too big for that."

But even as she spoke, she could hear Lauren's voice outside: "Melody, help me move this. We need to get to the second cache before —"

"ENOUGH!" Kale roared, and suddenly Melody was being dragged back through the door, Kale's arm around her throat and a gun pressed to her temple. "No more games. No more negotiations. Where is Charlie Joe's evidence?"

Melody's face was pale but determined. Her eyes met Jackie's steadily, and Jackie could see her niece's brilliant mind working even in this terrifying moment.

"The evidence is in the storm cellar," Melody said clearly. "Under the restaurant. Charlie Joe built a hidden room when he renovated the building."

Jackie felt her heart stop. There was no storm cellar. Melody was buying them time, but at what cost?

"Show me," Kale demanded.

"I'll show you," Lauren said, appearing in the doorway with her hands raised. "Let Melody go, and I'll take you to the evidence."

"Everyone goes," Kale said. "One happy family expedition."

That's when Tom Whitfield came crashing through the front window.

"Let the girl go!" he shouted, wielding what appeared to be a crowbar. But before he could reach Kale, FBI agents swarmed through the broken window behind him. How they got passed Kale's associates and the fire barrier was a mystery as Jackie had been so focused on Kale's face.

"Federal agents! Drop your weapon!"

"Whitfield, stand down!" Matt Klein's voice boomed as agents tackled Tom to the ground.

"I'm trying to help!" Tom protested as zip-ties secured his hands. "The girl's in danger!"

"You're compromising a federal operation!" Matt shouted back.

Kale's men came in the back door, guns drawn. There was a brief standoff, but in the end Matt ordered everyone out. The agents retreated back behind the fire barrier.

In the chaos, Kale tightened his grip on Melody and backed through the kitchen and out the back door. "Everyone out! Now! Or the girl dies and this place burns with Charlie Joe's secrets inside!"

Jackie's earpiece crackled, then went silent. The FBI's careful coordination was falling apart.

"Lauren," she said quietly, "we're on our own."

"What do we do?" Lauren whispered.

Jackie looked at her sister, then at Melody, who despite the gun at her head was still thinking, still planning. The three of them had spent weeks learning to work together, learning to trust each other's strengths.

"We finish what Uncle Charlie Joe started," Jackie said. "Melody, is there really a storm cellar?"

"No," Melody said calmly, "but there is a root cellar behind the building. And that's where Uncle Charlie Joe actually hid the evidence. I panicked earlier."

"You're lying," Kale said, but uncertainty crept into his voice.

"Uncle Charlie Joe documented everything," Melody continued in her matter-of-fact tone. "Including your conversation with Sheriff Henderson about making his death look natural. The recording device is in the root cellar, along with financial records going back to 1994."

Jackie felt a surge of admiration for her niece. Even terrified, Melody was using her systematic mind to feed Kale information that would make him desperate to reach the evidence.

"Take me there," Kale demanded. "All of you. Now."

As they moved toward the back door, Jackie caught Lauren's eye and mouthed silently: "Root cellar?"

Lauren nodded almost imperceptibly. There was indeed an old root cellar behind the restaurant, though Jackie had no idea if it contained evidence or not.

Outside, the smell of gasoline was overwhelming. Small fires ringed the building, and Jackie could see FBI agents maintaining their perimeter but unable to move closer without triggering a larger blaze.

She could hear Tom's voice protesting his innocence from somewhere in the dark.

"There," Lauren pointed to an area near the oak tree where old wooden doors were set into the ground. "Charlie Joe reinforced it when he bought the property."

Kale forced Melody ahead of him, keeping the gun pressed to her head as they approached the cellar doors. "Open it."

Lauren knelt and pulled up the heavy wooden doors, revealing stone steps leading down into darkness. The smell that emerged was musty and old but not threatening.

"You first," Kale told Jackie. "Then the mother. I keep the girl until I see what's down there."

Jackie descended the stone steps, Lauren close behind her. The cellar was larger than she'd expected, with stone walls and wooden shelving. And there, on a table in the center of the room, was a metal filing cabinet and what appeared to be recording equipment.

"It's here," Jackie called up. "The filing cabinet is locked, but the recording equipment is set up like he was documenting meetings."

Kale came down, leaving Melody above with one of his men. He looked around the space.

"Bring the girl down," Kale shouted to someone above. "And get lights down here."

As Melody was forced down the steps, Jackie noticed something that made her heart race. The recording equipment wasn't just set up, it was running. A small red light indicated it was actively recording.

Charlie Joe's final trap. The evidence wasn't just stored here; this room was designed to capture confessions from anyone who came looking for it.

"Open the filing cabinet," Kale demanded, releasing Melody to examine the equipment himself.

"It needs a key," Lauren said.

"Then find one!"

As they searched the cellar, Jackie realized that Charlie Joe had orchestrated this entire scenario. The root cellar wasn't just a hiding place, it was a confession booth, designed to record the words of whoever came seeking his evidence. Her niece was brilliant. How had she known this? But then Jackie remembered that Melody had explored the entire property since they'd arrived and had documented every bit of it.

"Mr. Kale," Melody said suddenly, "before you look at those files, you should know that Uncle Charlie Joe left a message specifically for you."

She pointed to a tape player separate from the recording equipment. "He said whoever came for his evidence would want to hear it first."

Kale's eyes gleamed with triumph and curiosity. "Play it."

Melody pressed play, and Uncle Charlie Joe's voice filled the stone chamber:

"Harrison, if you're hearing this, it means you've finally decided to clean up loose ends. You always were thorough about eliminating witnesses. But you see, I spent thirty years preparing for this moment, and I have one final surprise for you..."

The recording continued as Charlie Joe's voice calmly detailed Kale's crimes, his methods, his associates, and his plans. Information only the real killer could know, information that was being captured by the hidden recording system even as Kale listened to his own crimes being recited.

"How did he —" Kale began, then stopped as he realized the trap he'd walked into.

"Uncle Charlie Joe knew you'd come," Melody said simply. "He knew you'd want to hear what he'd documented. And he knew you'd confess while you were here, because he understood how criminals think."

Jackie felt overwhelming pride in her uncle's final strategy and in her niece's courage in executing it.

But Kale's response was swift and violent. "Then you'll all die with his secrets," he snarled, raising his gun.

That's when Lauren grabbed a pickaxe from the wall and swung it with desperate strength, not to hit Kale but to smash the lantern providing their only light.

In the sudden darkness, Jackie heard Melody's voice: "FBI! Now!"

The cellar exploded with light and shouting voices as federal agents poured down the steps. In the confusion, Jackie grabbed

Melody and Lauren, pulling them against the stone wall as the arrest unfolded around them.

When the dust settled, Harrison Kale and his men were all in handcuffs, the recording equipment had captured everything, and the three women were alive, shaken, but victorious.

"How did you know the FBI would come?" Jackie asked Melody as they emerged from the cellar.

"I didn't," Melody replied matter-of-factly. "But I knew Uncle Charlie Joe would have planned for this exact scenario. The recording system was motion-activated and transmitted directly to law enforcement. As soon as we entered the cellar, help was already coming."

Jackie looked at her sister and niece with overwhelming admiration. They had trusted each other, used their individual strengths, and finished what Uncle Charlie Joe had started.

"Is it over?" Lauren asked as they watched Kale being led away.

"It's over," Matt Klein confirmed, approaching with relief evident on his face. "Charlie Joe's final recording contains enough evidence to convict everyone in Kale's network. Including admissions Kale made while he was down there with you."

As FBI agents secured the scene, Jackie noticed Tom Whitfield being led away in handcuffs, shouting protests as agents searched his truck.

"What about Tom?" she asked Matt.

Matt's expression grew troubled. "We found professional surveillance equipment in his truck, detailed maps of your property, documentation of Charlie Joe's routines, and tracking logs of all your movements for the past two months. His truck also contained communications equipment that could have been used to coordinate with Kale's operation."

"But Tom was trying to help —" Lauren began.

"Tom Whitfield will be held pending a full investigation," Matt interrupted. "Right now, all evidence suggests he was providing intelligence to Kale's network. Whether he was a willing participant or being blackmailed, we'll determine during questioning."

Jackie watched Tom being loaded into a federal transport vehicle, his face a mask of confusion and anger. After everything they'd learned about his protective instincts, seeing him arrested as a suspected criminal felt wrong. But the evidence in his truck was damning.

"Sometimes the people trying to help cause the most problems," Matt said quietly. "Tom's surveillance may have been well-intentioned, but it provided Kale with exactly the intelligence he needed to plan tonight's operation."

As they stood in the aftermath of the confrontation, Dr. Thorne arrived at the restaurant. He looked lighter than they'd seen him since Uncle Charlie Joe's death.

"It's finished," he said simply. "The truth is finally out."

"How do you feel about that?" Lauren asked.

"Relieved. Guilty. Grateful." Dr. Thorne managed a small smile. "Mostly determined to never let fear of professional consequences override my medical obligations again."

"What happens now?" Melody asked.

"Now I provide whatever additional testimony is needed for the trials. I work with the state medical board to develop better protocols for handling suspicious deaths in rural communities. And I try to rebuild the trust this community placed in me." Dr. Thorne looked around the restaurant. "Starting with making sure Charlie Joe's family knows they have reliable medical care available."

"You'll stay in Prairie Rose?" Jackie asked.

"This community needs a doctor, and I need to prove I can be the doctor this community deserves." Dr. Thorne's voice grew stronger. "Charlie Joe believed in second chances, in people being able to make amends for their mistakes. I'd like to honor that belief."

Chapter Twenty-One

About a week after the arrest of Harrison Kale and the dismantling of his criminal network, Prairie Rose was buzzing with a different kind of excitement. News crews had come and gone, federal investigators had finished processing evidence, and life was slowly returning to something resembling normal.

But normal, Jackie was discovering, now included being minor celebrities in the law enforcement community and around the Texas Hill Country.

"Another interview request," Lauren announced, hanging up the restaurant phone. "This time from *Texas Monthly*. They want to do a feature story about the family that helped solve a thirty-year-old federal case."

"Can we just serve barbecue in peace?" Jackie asked, though she was smiling as she said it. The attention had been overwhelming, but it had also brought something unexpected: a sense of closure and pride in what they'd accomplished.

"Not likely," said Matt Klein, entering through the front door. It wasn't quite lunch time, but since the arrest, he'd become a regular customer and an unofficial family friend. "The FBI Director wants to present you with civilian service awards next month."

"Awards?" Melody looked up from her laptop where she was updating their newly expanded catering menu. "For what? We just answered questions honestly."

"You did more than that. You helped bring down the largest money laundering operation in Southwest history," Matt reminded her. "Kale's network was responsible for cleaning over two billion dollars in illegal money over four decades. Your courage in facing him down made it possible to get his full confession on record."

Jackie still couldn't quite believe it was over. The man who had killed Uncle Charlie Joe, who had terrorized their family for months, was now facing life in prison without the possibility of parole. Along with forty-seven associates who had been arrested in coordinated raids across six states, including Sheriff Henderson for his role in covering up murder.

She couldn't believe how large the operation was. It was one of the biggest cases she'd seen.

"Dr. Thorne's report was essential to our case," Matt explained. "His detailed observations, combined with his willingness to admit his earlier mistakes, provided the medical foundation we needed to charge Kale with murder rather than just financial crimes."

"Will Dr. Thorne face any professional consequences for his earlier decisions?" Lauren asked.

"The state medical board will review his actions, but his cooperation with our investigation and his detailed documentation of the pressure he faced will likely result in additional training requirements rather than loss of license," Matt replied. "Dr. Thorne's willingness to come forward actually helped us identify similar patterns in other jurisdictions where local medical professionals were pressured to avoid thorough death investigations."

"Other cases?" Jackie asked.

"Henderson wasn't just covering up Charles's murder. He was part of a network that used intimidation of medical professionals to hide evidence of multiple crimes across rural Texas," Matt said. "Dr. Thorne's testimony will help us prosecute several other cases where suspicious deaths were incorrectly ruled natural causes."

"I hope it can bring Dr. Thorne some peace and he doesn't face any negative impact. He really is a good man who made bad choices," Jackie said with a smile. "Oh, by the way, Ruth Pemberton stopped by yesterday. She wanted to think us for helping."

"I know she was feeling a lot of guilt for her part in things." Matt smiled. "She really is a sweet lady."

"She really didn't do anything to us. She was pleasant when she came in, and didn't make any threats," Lauren said.

"And what about Gerald? Will he be released?" Jackie asked.

"He'll have a new trial, but I think the chances are good he'll be found innocent."

"That's good."

"I also wanted to let you know that Tom's been released," Matt announced.

"What?" Jackie, Lauren, and Melody said simultaneously.

"Turns out Tom wasn't working with Kale's organization. He was working against them."

"What do you mean?" Lauren asked.

Matt sat down heavily. "Tom's been conducting his own investigation into Charles's death for the past six months or more. Right about the time Charles started getting paranoid and strangers started showing up in town. Tom knew something wasn't right. All that surveillance equipment, the detailed mapping, the close monitoring of your routines, he was trying to protect you, not harm you."

"Protect us?" Jackie asked incredulously.

"Tom figured out that Charles had been murdered, and he was worried the same people would come after his family. All his harassment, all the business sabotage, it was designed to make you sell the property and get you to safety before the real killers showed up."

"By making our lives miserable?" Lauren asked. "That doesn't make sense."

"By trying to force you to leave before you got killed," Matt corrected. "Tom's not good at expressing concern in healthy ways, but he was genuinely trying to save your lives."

"Then why didn't he just tell us about the danger?" Jackie asked.

"Because Tom Whitfield is a fifty-six-year-old rancher who doesn't trust law enforcement, doesn't believe in involving outsiders in local problems, and thought he could handle a murder investigation by himself." Matt shook his head. "Classic cowboy mentality to protect people by making their decisions for them instead of giving them information and letting them choose."

"So, all his threats, all his comments about accidents happening..." Jackie began.

"His sabotages," Lauren added.

"Were his clumsy way of trying to warn you that you were in real danger without admitting he couldn't protect you from professional killers." Matt pulled out a folder. "Tom documented everything from suspicious vehicles, strangers asking questions in town, evidence of surveillance around your property. He's been building a case file for months."

"And the cattle in our parking lot? The contaminated water?" Melody asked.

"Desperate attempts to create business failures that would force you to sell before Kale's people made their move." Matt smiled ruefully. "Tom was so focused on getting you to leave that he never considered the possibility of helping you stay and fight."

"He really thought he was protecting us?" Lauren asked.

Matt nodded. "Tom Whitfield has been the unofficial protector of this area for thirty years and his family has been at it for longer. When he realized professional killers were circling his neighbors' property, his instinct was to handle it the way he'd handle any threat to the community, by removing the vulnerable people from danger."

Jackie felt a complex mix of relief, guilt, and frustrated affection. "So, Tom's not a criminal conspirator. He's just a well-meaning control freak with terrible communication skills."

"And a thirty-year grudge about land that made us assume the worst about his motives," Lauren added.

"Family land disputes have a way of poisoning relationships," Matt observed. "Tom's grandfather really did have a handshake agreement to buy your property. Charlie Joe's cash offer disrupted their family's expansion plans. But Tom's spent thirty years living next to Charlie Joe without ever trying to hurt him which should have told us something about his actual character."

"We need to apologize," Jackie said. "And thank him. His surveillance probably helped provide evidence that led to Kale's arrest."

"Tom's waiting outside," Matt said. "He wanted to explain himself properly. I had told him he shouldn't do it alone, so I came with him."

They found Tom Whitfield standing beside his truck, hat in his hands, looking as though he'd aged ten years and more vulnerable than they'd ever seen him.

"Ladies," he said quietly. "I owe you an apology and an explanation."

"Tom," Jackie began, but he held up his hand.

"Let me say my piece first. I handled this all wrong. I knew you were in danger, and instead of treating you like capable adults who could make their own decisions, I tried to manipulate you into leaving. That was wrong of me."

"You were trying to protect us," Lauren said gently.

"I was trying to control a situation I didn't understand well enough to control," Tom corrected. "My daddy always said the Whitfield way was to take action first and explain later. That approach doesn't work so well when you're dealing with federal criminal conspiracies, but all I knew for sure was there were strangers threatening my neighbors and I had to do something."

"Your surveillance helped catch the real criminals," Melody pointed out.

"Maybe. But it also made your lives hell when I should have been honest about the danger and asked how I could help you face it." Tom looked directly at each of them. "Charlie Joe was a good neighbor. I didn't appreciate that when he was alive, and I compounded that mistake by not trusting his family to be as strong and smart as he was."

"Apology accepted," Jackie said. "And Tom? If you really want to make amends, I have a proposition for you."

"What kind of proposition?"

"We're planning to expand the restaurant, maybe add some outdoor activities, educational programs about Hill Country agriculture on the weekends." Jackie smiled. "We could use a partner who understands ranching, someone who could help us create programs that honor both the land's agricultural heritage and its current use as a community gathering place."

Tom's eyes widened. "You'd want to work with me? After everything I put you through?"

"We'd want to work with someone who cares enough about this community to spend months conducting his own murder investigation to protect his neighbors," Lauren said. "Even if his methods were questionable."

"Plus," Melody added, "your generational knowledge of this land combined with our business and therapeutic expertise could create educational programs with significant community value."

Tom was quiet for a long moment, processing the unexpected offer of partnership instead of punishment.

"I'd be honored," he said finally. "And I promise, no more cattle in your parking lot."

"Though we might want to add some educational cattle demonstrations," Jackie said with a grin. "Properly scheduled ones, of course."

"Of course, of course." He chuckled.

As Tom drove away with a lighter expression than they'd seen from him in months, Matt Klein shook his head in amazement.

"Charlie Joe would be proud," he said. "You just turned your biggest antagonist into your strongest ally."

"We turned a frightened neighbor who didn't know how to ask for help into a community partner," Lauren corrected. "That's what family restaurants do. They bring people together instead of driving them apart."

"Even people who contaminate our water supply?" Melody asked dryly.

"Especially people who contaminate our water supply," Jackie laughed. "If we can forgive cattle-based harassment, we can probably forgive anything."

"So, Matt, any word on the trial timeline?" Lauren asked.

"With the evidence Charlie Joe compiled and Kale's recorded confession, most of them are taking plea deals," Matt said. "The few who want to fight it will face trial next year, but the outcome isn't really in doubt."

"Good," Jackie said firmly. "Uncle Charlie Joe deserves justice. And so do all the other people they hurt."

The front door chimed, and Sheriff Martinez entered, looking more relaxed than Jackie had seen him since the night of the arrests.

"Morning, folks. Just wanted to make sure you knew that the FBI finished processing the evidence from your property. You're free to use the land however you want now."

"Yep, Matt told us already," Jackie said.

"Smart of Charlie Joe to bury all of that under the oak tree," Martinez explained. "Financial records going back forty years, recorded conversations with Kale's associates, photographs of murders being planned. It was the final piece that connected all the crimes. Amazing that it was right there the whole time."

"Uncle Charlie Joe really did think of everything," Melody observed.

"He spent thirty years preparing for that confrontation," Matt said. "He knew eventually Kale would come for him, and he wanted to make sure his family would be safe, and his evidence would see the light of day."

"Speaking of family," Martinez said, looking directly at Lauren, "I was wondering if you'd like to have dinner. Now that life has calmed down a bit."

Lauren felt her cheeks warm. The chaos of the federal investigation had put any romantic thoughts on hold, but now that the dust was settling, she found herself very interested in exploring what might develop between them.

"I'd love that," she said. "Though I should warn you, I'll probably spend the entire evening talking about restaurant business."

"I'm counting on it," Martinez replied with a grin. "I'll call you later."

After he left, the phone rang again. Lauren answered.

"Another catering request," Lauren announced, hanging up the restaurant phone. "This time from the Fredericksburg Chamber of Commerce. They want us to cater their annual awards dinner for two hundred people."

"Two hundred people?" Jackie looked up from the supply orders she'd been reviewing. "That's our biggest request yet."

"And they're willing to pay premium prices for what they're calling 'the barbecue that brought down a criminal empire,'" Lauren added with a laugh.

Melody looked up from her laptop where she was designing logistics workflows for their expanding catering operations. "We've received fourteen catering requests this week. Corporate events, weddings, family reunions, church functions. The publicity from Uncle Charlie Joe's case has created significant demand for our services."

Jackie still couldn't quite believe how much their lives had changed. The restaurant that had once struggled to serve thirty customers on a busy day was now booking catering events months in advance.

"I've been getting the calls too. Event planners from Austin and San Antonio wanting to partner with us for Hill Country destination events. The combination of authentic barbecue and dramatic backstory makes for compelling marketing," Matt observed.

"People want to eat food prepared by the women who helped solve a thirty-year-old murder case and I'm happy to partner with you. And now that my biggest case is closed, I can simply enjoy my retirement doing what I enjoy most."

The growth had been overwhelming but exciting. Their Sunday community dinners had evolved into a local institution, but they'd also discovered that their systematic approach to large-scale cooking made them naturals for catering events.

"The secret is Melody's logistics systems," Jackie explained to anyone who asked about their success. "She's turned barbecue catering into a precise science."

"Optimal timing calculations for multiple protein types, systematic workflow management, and scalable preparation protocols," Melody said, consulting her ever-present notebook. "Plus, quality control measures that ensure consistency regardless of event size."

"Translation: she's figured out how to serve perfect barbecue to three hundred people while making it look effortless," Lauren added with pride.

Their catering success had allowed them to hire additional staff. Maria Santos had become their full-time catering coordinator, and they'd brought in three more prep cooks and two servers for large events.

"We're becoming a real business," Jackie marveled during their weekly planning meeting. "With employees and equipment loans and health insurance."

"We're becoming Uncle Charlie Joe's dream realized," Lauren corrected. "A place that brings people together through great food, just on a larger scale than he probably imagined."

"And we've learned to be in the same room for more than twenty minutes without fighting," Jackie said.

"Yes, we can now go a whole twenty-one minutes!"

They laughed. It was a good feeling for the two sisters to finally become what they had been missing; family working together, supporting each other and not taking sides.

Jackie knew that Uncle Charlie Joe would be so proud.

They just didn't know at the time that their next challenge would arrive via the U.S. Postal service later that day. For now, they would enjoy their small victory.

THE END

Before you go: If you loved Smoky Secrets, be sure to visit my website to sign up for my newsletter and to stay up to date on new releases and other bookish things. When signing up, you can pick either Unsolved Murder, prequel to my Medium with a Heart series, or the Alphabet Soup Recipe from my Alphabet Soup Mysteries series. Either are a win.

Continue to the next section for this book's recipe!

www.ejwheltonwrites.com

Recipe:

I wanted to share a fun side dish that is easy and goes beautifully with barbecue. I learned how to make coleslaw from my first mother-in-law. She was the sweetest lady, a great cook, and a loving MIL and grandmother to my children. She passed away years ago, and even though that first marriage didn't stick, I loved her very much and miss her every day.

I have tweaked the recipe over the years, but the basic is what she taught me.

Coleslaw:

7-8 cups cabbage
½ - 1 cup shredded carrots
Or,
1 prepackaged coleslaw mix (the one I buy is 7 ½ cups)
1 cup mayonnaise
1 tablespoon red wine vinegar (or any vinegar)
1 tablespoon white sugar
½ teaspoon salt
½ teaspoon celery salt
½ teaspoon dill
½ teaspoon black pepper (optional)

Mix dry ingredients with coleslaw mix then add mayonnaise and vinegar. Mix until combined. Then, put in a container with a tight-fitting lid and shake it until mixed.

Chill in refrigerator for at least 4 hours (or longer), stirring/shaking occasionally. Enjoy!!

Author note:

This story has been swimming in my head for a while just hoping I would sit and write it down. I finally did and the characters cheered!

The characters are very special to me. I'm not sure why but I felt like one of them. Melody is especially dear to my heart. She is a blend of my three grandsons who are all autistic and at different places on the spectrum. They are still young boys, but I can really imagine them growing to be a lot like her, especially my oldest grandson.

He is always going through tons of paper, drawing constantly. He is very analytically-minded, and all three of them research their interests and can quote facts all day long about those topics.

Anyway, I hope you enjoyed it! Until next time, happy reading.

www.ejwheltonwrites.com

www.ingramcontent.com/pod-product-compliance
Lightning Source LLC
Chambersburg PA
CBHW022212050726
47590CB00002B/765